BOUNDARY

EBONY OLSON

ALSO BY EBONY OLSON

Hotel Series

Henderson

Cassidy

Holmes

Best Man

Black Mark Series

Black Mark's Resistance

Black Mark's Secret

Black Mark's Heart

Black Mark: The Complete Saga

Angelis Series

Spectra

Hierarch Series

Succumb

Numinous

Masked

Standalones

Of Shadow and Light

EBANDMUSE
PUBLICATIONS

Published 2019
Published by
EbandMuse Publications
Sydney, Australia

Copyright © 2017 by **Ebony Olson.**

ISBN: 978-0-6485000-6-3

http://ebonyolson.com/

CHAPTER 1

*T*he cottage was perfect. From the moment I paid the settlement fee until I arrived this morning to pick up the keys, I worried it was a con. But it was even prettier than in the pictures. Now, I had to hope the inside wasn't derelict.

A gaudy yellow high-end sports car pulled up beside me, and a man in a designer suit stepped out. After checking his styled blond hair in the mirror of his car, he walked to me. "Good morning, are you Ms. Cana's daughter?"

Raising a brow at the assumption, I folded my arms across my chest. "No. I am Miss Cana."

Brows jumping, the man's eyes widened as he looked me over. "Really? I was expecting an older woman to want a cottage like this."

At twenty-eight, I wasn't too young to own my own home. "Yes, my name is Vera Cana, and I purchased the cottage." For the first time in years, I didn't have to force my smile. Not that this egotistical man caused it. The cottage and the keys to it that this man was holding gifted me this joy.

Grinning, his eyes traveled over me a second time. It wasn't lecherous, there was nothing to see. My long sleeved teal boat neck top covered my breasts, and the loose black slacks went all the way to my ballet flats. Since I couldn't be bothered straightening it today, my mahogany wavy hair was up in a bun. I wore no makeup, so my skin was my natural alabaster, something my ex didn't find attractive.

That was my look now, neat, put together, but as unattractive to the opposite sex as I could be. Danny Ready perused my appearance, then frowned and returned his eyes to my fake muddy brown ones. My eyes were actually a vivid green; a feature men tended to pay attention too. To be unremarkable, the eyes needed to stay hidden.

"Well, it's nice to finally meet you. I'm Danny Ready. Your real estate agent's representative here since they don't have an office down this way." Danny held up the keys. "Here are the keys to your new home, Miss Cana. Should we look inside to make sure it's what you purchased?"

Taking the keys, I met his eyes again. "Is it furnished still?"

"Yes, of course, that was part of the sale contract. Mr. Ways son only removed personal effects and memorabilia. Even the crockery and cutlery remain in case you wanted that."

Grateful, I smiled. I'd spent the vast majority of my savings on the purchase of the land, and I didn't want to have to buy anything to move in.

"Excellent, well, I can take it from here, Mr. Ready. Thank you." Turning my back on him, I moved to collect my bag from my second hand, but immaculate coupe.

"Would you like me to help you with your things?"

When Mr. Ready followed me to my car, I huffed. Forcing my well-rehearsed smile, I turned back. "No, I only have my overnight bag. The rest of my belongings will follow." Lie.

"Oh. Well, very well then." Danny handed me his business card. "If you need anything, or have any questions, don't hesitate to call."

With a nod, I accepted his card then turned my back on him again. Frowning in the reflection of my car window, Danny turned away. Collecting my handbag from the passenger seat of my car, I closed and locked the door as I moved to the boot.

Revving his sports car, Danny Ready drove back up the long drive. The cottage was on the grounds of a historic manor house and used to belong to the owner's loyal butler. The bungalow and land gifted to him by the owner for his service.

Danny had told me the butler served two generations of the family before he died at age eighty-three. His son left for college as a teen and never returned, and the wife passed thirty years ago. The son listed it for sale without even offering the estate owner the chance to repurchase it.

The listing went live at the same moment I was looking for a perfect out of the way place, and I'd bought it within the hour. The owner of the manor house hadn't been happy the cottage sold. His lawyer emailed me a few weeks ago and tried to reverse the sale.

This caused a two-week delay in taking possession. Our lawyers examined the deeds and determined that, yes, I now owned the cottage. There was nothing Mr. Hern could do about the sale. The extra expense it cost me in legal fees obliterated the rest of my savings, but at least the cottage was mine.

Grabbing the overnight case and the two bags of food I'd bought on the way here, I looked out over the cottage. The deeds gave me the bungalow, the acre of cleared land around it, and the driveway. The forest surrounding my allotment belonged to the manor house. The real estate agent told me the woods were full of deer and rabbit, and the previous owner had been free to use it.

Of course, that was before the owner tried to steal the cottage back from me. He would likely have me charged with trespass if he caught me wandering the woods around his home now. Then again, Mr. Hearn lived and worked in the city, three hours away from here and only came home on the weekends. So, there might be some room for movement.

Unlocking the front door of the cottage, I stepped inside. My smile bloomed. The place was perfect. A simplistic single story with a well-orchestrated floor plan. The long, wide hall displayed art and landscape photographs.

There were two large bedrooms to either side of the entrance hall, each with a walk-in closet and bathroom. Walking into the master bedroom, I deposited the suitcase containing my only belongings. Then headed off to find the kitchen to put my groceries away.

The open living area in the rear of the cottage contained the kitchen and lounge. The floor to ceiling glass windows overlooked the yard, the forest, and the veranda off of the living area. The cottage was beautiful, and everything I needed.

After a few minutes of unpacking, I spent the rest of the afternoon getting acquainted with my new home.

Opening my laptop, I connected it out to the internet. The technicians came out earlier this week to set the cottage up with high-speed internet. It was another costly venture, but since it provided my income, it's what I needed more than clothes.

Making myself a small salad for dinner, I toasted my new home and life with a small glass of wine. After supper, I showered and changed into the only pair of pajamas I owned; a little black singlet and short set. Wrapping my long black dressing gown around me, I walked out onto the back deck to overlook the yard.

The lights around the perimeter of the yard were aglow, though I hadn't switched them on. There was a path of lights leading into the forest from the yard. Assessing their direction, I decided it led to the main house. More than likely created to enable the butler to get home in the dark.

Feeling brave, since it was the middle of the week, I stepped off the back porch and wandered along the path. The trees were dense, and the smell of wood and earth suffused my senses.

An animal noise made me stop. Peering to my left, I spied a small pond and a doe drinking from it. Moving off the path towards it, I kept low and quiet. Having never seen a live deer before, I was curious how tame the animals were here.

The doe lifted her head to watch me approach. "It's okay, I'm not going to hurt you. I'll stay on this side of the pond. I just want to watch you."

The doe hesitated but allowed me to come closer. When I reached this side of the pond, I squatted to watch it, tucking my robe around my legs so it wouldn't get in the dirt. The doe and I sat staring at each other, my smile growing.

Then the doe cocked her head, eyes widened with fright, and she darted off into the forest. Standing surprised, I wondered what startled her. Turning my attention to where the doe spooked, it took me a moment to see the golden eyes reflecting the moonlight in the dark.

Swallowing the lump of fear in my throat, I took a step back as the snout of the dog became clearer. "Nice puppy." My voice trembled like my legs as adrenaline coursed through my veins.

The dog snarled, it's lip lifting to show enormous canines. Backing up, I exhaled hard when I rammed straight into a tree. Cringing with the pain that burst through my already injured side, I prayed that this was a dog from the main house. "Okay, not a puppy. Nice doggy?"

The animal lifted itself from the foliage and stepped into the clear, allowing me to see it. It lowered its large head and snarled again as it evened its weight on its paws. Knowing that maneuver from the discovery channel, I tried to plot my retreat while keeping an eye on the dog.

The animal was huge, and it took me another moment to realize, it wasn't a domestic dog breed I'd ever seen before. "Oh, god. Not a nice doggy then."

Bolting through the forest towards the cottage, I used the lights of the path off to my left to guide me. The snarling and snapping of foliage let me know the dog was chasing me through the scrub, gaining on me.

Making the clearing, I tripped on a cable I hadn't seen before. Falling to the ground with a yelp, I caught myself on my hands. Refusing to take the time to feel the cut across my shin from the cable, or the fact breathing hurt, I rolled over. Sprawled on the ground, I stared at the angry dog as it slowed and crossed the boundary of my land.

It snarled at me again, stalking closer. Whimpering, I cringed back as it lunged for me. Snatching my dressing gown, the dog tried to drag me back to the forest. Clinging to the ground, I dug my fingers in to try and prevent it pulling me to my death.

When material started ripping, I realized it gave me an opportunity. Letting go of the ground, I yanked the tie on the robe and shrugged out of it. Sobbing as I backed away, I crawled further into the yard toward the cottage. My ankle was on fire, so trying to stand and take my weight would only disable me.

Growling, the dog swung his head, throwing my gown to the side before he lunged forward. Throwing my arms up to protect me, I prepared for the worst. Nothing happened.

The dog was standing above me, his breathing angry, but it didn't bite me. Opening my eyes, I dared a peek. Standing astride my legs, it was staring at my body, then lowering his snout to my exposed abdomen, the dog sniffed.

Whimpering when he poked the freshly healed wound in my side, I cringed. The stitches only came out last week. He nuzzled the bruising across my abdomen, causing me to sob louder.

Stepping back, the dog nuzzled the dark bruises across my thighs. Lifting its head, the dog frowned at me, tilting his head in question. Biting my lip on the fear inside me, I found the sudden pity in the beast's eyes disturbing. Waiting, he barked at me before poking my bruised thigh.

"You're not the first beast to attack me." Trembling, I pulled myself out from under him and glared into his eyes. I swear they'd changed. Not so gold anymore, not so animal.

The dog backed up a step, then another. Turning to consider the forest, it then glared back at me. With an undercurrent of growl, it snapped towards me.

Jumping, I whimpered, nodding my head. "Stay out of the forest. I get it."

With another growl, the dog turned and leaped over the cable I'd not seen, and back into the forest. Sobbing as the night became quiet around me again, I collapsed and bawled into my forearm.

I'd survived years of abuse and risked death to earn my freedom. To near die at the jaws of a wild animal on my first night of freedom was too much. Fate could be cruel.

CHAPTER 2

Sitting at the dining table working, I was enjoying a coffee as the light of day revealed the world outside. Pressing send on my latest project to my client, I was closing my laptop when there was a knock at the front door.

It'd been three days since I moved in and made the mistake of entering the forest. The cut to my shin had been superficial, but my ankle was still tricky to walk on. Unfortunately, it was also my right ankle. That meant driving wasn't an option until I could apply weight to it.

Hesitant, I hopped to the front door, then opened it only a crack. A man in khaki shorts, a polo shirt, and grass-stained work boots stood on the porch. His smile was friendly as he took in my loose slacks and flowing grey singlet top. His blue eyes met my brown contacts, and he took off his hat to expose honey blond hair.

"Morning. I'm Bob, the groundskeeper for the manor house."

Easing the door opened a little further, I checked there was no one else with him. "Morning."

When I stood watching him with the door only half open, Bob smirked. "I've been taking care of the grounds here too for the last few years. Mr. Hearn used to pay for it, but now that it's sold, he's told me to negotiate with the new owner for my services."

It took me a moment, then I finally caught on. "Oh. I'm not sure. I mean, I hadn't even considered having someone maintain it for me." My gaze dropped to his work boots. Damn it, I'd not accounted for any of this. After doing the maths, I shook my head. "I'm afraid I can't afford your services, Bob. I'm sorry."

His eyes assessing me now, Bob frowned. "Are you a keen gardener?"

"No. I love nature and plants, hence why I bought the place, but I've never had to care for any myself."

Stepping back and looking back up the drive, Bob sighed then met my eyes again. "This place will be overgrown and ruined in months if you don't keep up with it. What can you afford to pay?"

Very friggin little thanks to Mr. Hearn and his lawyers. "Um, well, how much would you charge Mr. Hearn?"

"It was always included in the cost of the manor house. I guess, a grand a month would cover it." When I balked, Bob frowned. "Could you afford seven fifty?"

If I didn't want to eat or have functioning electricity. "I'd have to do the sums. Can you drop by tomorrow?"

"Sure. I'm happy to negotiate." He turned to leave.

"Bob?" Opening the door, I limped out onto the porch.

Bob turned back, noticed my limping and frowned. "You're hurt?" He reached for me.

Terror froze my heart, and I stepped back as an automatic reaction. My ankle didn't hold, and I cried out as I fell to the porch. Bob tried to take my arm, but I cowered in fear and pulled back from him. That made Bob stop. He stepped back, his blue eyes wide as he watched me.

Cursing under my breath, I shuffled back against the wall and stabilized my breathing. "I'm sorry, I just... don't touch me, okay?"

"Okay." Bob took another step back.

Gritting my teeth, I looked away, unable to meet his eyes. "I wanted to know if the local store delivered groceries by any chance? I can't drive till my ankle heals and I'm running out of food."

Bob shook his head. "No, they don't. It's only a small grocery store. None of the big chains have bothered coming out this way yet."

Figuring that was the case, I slumped back against the front wall of the house. "Thanks."

Bob licked his lips. "Look, the new butler, he does shopping for Mr. Hearn. If you write me a list and give me the cash, I'm sure he would pick up what you need until your ankle heals." Peering up, I meet Bob's eyes, unsure. "Trust isn't your strong suit, huh?"

I shook my head.

Squatting so he was level with me, Bob sighed. He wasn't a tall man, close to the same height as me. "Look, Mr. Hearn isn't around a lot. Even when he is, he's not too concerned with what his staff is doing. As long as we take care of the place, he has other priorities. Jeremy and I, we can help you out for a few weeks. We don't mind."

"Jeremy is the butler?"

"We won't hurt you. I'll take care of the grounds, and Jeremy will drop off your groceries. You don't have to interact with us if it troubles you."

In my heart, I wanted to believe him, but my past experiences of men had never ended well. The man seemed genuine, and something about Bob appealed to me, apart from his looks.

When I continued staring at my knees, Bob sighed and dropped his eyes to his toes. "Is it only men?" My head snapped up to appraise his question. "That you fear? Is it only men?"

Hesitating only a moment, I gave a small nod.

"If I told you I was neutered and posed no threat to you, would you allow me to help you?"

Keeping my wide eyes low, I wondered if he was honest about his condition.

"Would you let me help you back inside? You can give me that list, and I'll see what I can organize for you?"

Closing my eyes, I took a deep breath. What other option did I have? When I held out my arm, Bob moved forward and wrapped my arm over his shoulder. My eyes went wide, and I squeaked when he pulled me into his arms like a groom would his bride.

"It's okay, I've got you." Bob carried me inside with ease.

Setting me on the lounge, he went to the freezer and put together an ice pack before coming back to me. Before I could protest, he lifted my trouser leg to wrap my ankle.

Sitting there wide-eyed, I wasn't sure how I should feel about his touching me. Once he'd wrapped my ankle, Bob's eyes went to the cut across my shin. Brows furrowing as he studied it, Bob used his finger to test the scab was holding. "How did you hurt yourself?"

"My first night here, I went for a walk. A large dog chased and attacked me. I tripped on the cable around the boundary."

"A large black dog?"

"Yes. How did you know? Is it from the manor house?"

"Yes. How did it attack you?"

My lip tremored as I recounted what happened. I didn't tell Bob about the dog's intelligence, or that when it saw my existing injuries, it backed away.

Rubbing the back of his head, Bob spotted a notepad and pen and brought it over to me. "Write me that list."

Taking the pad, I wrote out some generic food items I needed.

Taking the list when I finished, Bob huffed at it. "This is a pretty basic list, the only specific thing is the coffee."

"Good coffee is my only vice."

Ripping the list from the pad, Bob dropped the pen and pad back to the table. "I'll take care of this for you. Rest that ankle up." Making his way back out, I heard him set the lock before shutting the door, locking himself out. Turning my head to gaze out the window at the backyard, I sighed. My eyes felt heavy, so I closed them and slept.

A few hours later, I woke up and removed the now melted ice pack from my ankle. Limping over to the table and my computer, I had a few more clients waiting for their website packages. It would seem I needed the extra money sooner than later.

It wasn't until the next morning that I heard from anyone. There was a quiet knock at the front door mid-morning. Expecting Bob, I opened the door. Another man in his mid-thirties, with dirty blond hair, and a nice suit was unloading bags from a black Mercedes.

Glancing at the bags on the porch, I frowned. "This is more than on the list."

"I know." Shutting the boot, the man brought the last bag forward. "I added a few extra staples to your shopping." Meeting my eyes with his dark brown ones, he lifted a brow. "I'm Jeremy." When I nodded, he frowned. "This is usually the part where you introduce yourself."

"Vera."

Picking up the bags, Jeremy moved forward, making me shift back as he stepped into my home. Pressing myself against the wall, I held my breath as he passed. Jeremy's eyes turned fierce, his jaw tightened, but he said nothing else. Once he passed, I went to my room and collected my purse. Limping out to the kitchen, I saw Jeremy unpacking all the shopping.

"I can do that. How much do I owe you?"

"Was it your husband?"

My mouth fell open. "I, I don't know what you mean?"

"The man who beat you; who made you so afraid. Was it your husband?"

Gaping like a fish at his brazenness, I blinked. "I've never married."

"Ex-boyfriend?"

"Never had one of those either. How much do I owe you?"

"So it was your father?" Ignoring me, Jeremy kept unpacking.

"No! Please stop asking questions and tell me how much I owe you!" Closing the fridge, Jeremy studied me for a long moment. With a huff, he picked up the shopping bags and strode to the front door. "Wait, how much...?"

"Stop asking questions and get off that leg, Vera Cana." The door should have slammed with his tone of voice, but it closed with a quiet click.

Unsure what just happened, I stared at the door for several minutes. Clearing my throat, I put my purse on the counter then moved to the fridge. Noting the new items, I added up the cost.

Thirty minutes later, I heard a whipper sniper and looked up from my computer to see Bob working on the garden. Damn it! We still hadn't agreed on a price. Using the table to help me stand, I limped out onto the patio. "Bob!"

Glancing up, Bob turned off the tool and strode towards me. "Morning, how's the ankle?"

"Still sore. Can we talk about your costing?"

"Sure. What did you work out?"

"I can't afford anywhere near what you're asking. The most I could pay is half that, so if you could tend the lawns, I'll try and take care of the plants."

Bob kept smiling. "I tell you what, let's make it three hundred a month cash, and I'll still do the lot."

"That's very generous but unfair to you."

"Well, if you feel that way, we can always come to another agreement. Exchange your services for mine?" Any gratitude I had for him vanished immediately. Seeing it, Bob backpeddled. "Not those sort of services, Vera. I was thinking more mending tears in my clothes or doing my laundry. That sort of thing." Bob rubbed the back of his head. "Jesus, I would never ask a woman to do that other than for love or pleasure."

Shifting my stance, I stepped back inside and grabbed the money I'd put in an envelope. Limping back out, I placed the cash on the patio. Cringing at the tightness in my side, I held the still healing wound as I straightened. Bob's eyes narrowed in on my ribs.

"I'm afraid I'm useless in any way you'd benefit. Here is the money I owe for the shopping. Thank you for your kindness, but I'll manage on my own." Not waiting for a reply, I turned and limped back inside.

"Vera, wait?!"

Locking the door, I limped to my room. Steadying myself on the door frame to my bathroom, I swiped at the tears running down my face. My hand moved down of its own accord, into the band of my pants and rubbed over the raised flesh on my hip. The brand of my ownership to a pack of men.

Since I was a toddler, so young I couldn't even remember the face of my mother, I spent my childhood as their servant. Beautiful women would come and go from the estate. They always looked so lovely, got to wear pretty dresses, and treated like queens. I'd been invisible in the house until he came. Oh, how I wish I'd escaped the day he arrived.

Jumping free of my memories when the whipper sniper started again, anger grated on me. Why couldn't Bob leave? My ankle hurt, and I was exhausted from worrying about this new development, I laid down on my bed. I'd not counted on this. When I'd seen the cottage for sale, all I'd seen was a small house I could afford. A place isolated and away from the world. A safe home where I could live out my days in peace.

Now there were expenses I'd not accounted for in my budget. I wasn't meant to have money, so I'd never had bills to pay before. Homeschooled, at age ten the alpha had an outsider come in and train me up in graphics and web design.

From then on, I'd handled the web design of several of the brother's businesses. The freedom they gave me to perform that task enabled me to learn what life was like for others.

Not long after, I stumbled upon a site where you could offer your services for hire. Using a fake name and credentials that I traded from someone else on the site, I opened a bank account online. Using that same false name, I started developing web pages for other clients.

Eighteen years I'd worked and earned my own income below the table. Initially, I thought it would be nice to have in case I ever wanted to buy myself something. When I was fourteen, and he took over the pack, it became my escape plan.

CHAPTER 3

*I*t took two months for bob to wear me down. He came every week to do the gardening, and Jeremy was still doing my shopping for me, even though I'd recovered. Even when I went into town to do my own shopping, he'd always turn up with what he thought I needed. After a fortnight, I gave up and let him.

As summer came on, I felt sorry for Bob out there in the heat. Sighing in resignation, I poured him a large glass of water with ice and walked out onto the back porch. Glancing up from where he was clipping the hedge around the patio, Bob smiled. "Well, you finally came to say hello."

Placing the glass of water on the step, I moved back. "I thought you might be thirsty." Hurrying back inside, I shut and locked the screen door watching Bob come up the stairs from the safety of my house.

"You're like a puppy at a new place with bigger dogs."

"Literally! Does that dog always wander the property unattended?"

"You've seen him since?"

"A few times a week. He comes down and sits on the other side of the boundary for a while and then takes off."

Eyebrows lifting, Bob tilted his head a little. "Really? Just sits there, watching you?"

Was that weird for a dog? "I guess."

"Have you tried making friends with him?"

Huffing at the idea, I rolled my eyes. "The dog attacked me."

A glimmer in Bob's eyes made them an even brighter blue, then his lips lifted in the most swoon-worthy smirk. "You were a stranger then. Now, he's gotten used to you. Try making friends."

"How would I do that?"

Finishing his drink, Bob considered me. "Have you never had a pet?" Dropping my gaze to my feet, I shook my head. Bob frowned in my peripheral. Raising the empty glass as he put it back on the patio, Bob cocked a brow in my direction. "Try offering him a drink, and something to eat, but don't stay standing by the bowl. Put it out for him, then come sit on the steps. Let him approach you when he's ready."

"The last time he approached me, I ended up injured, remember?"

Eyes grazing over my ankle, Bob grimaced. "You were the trespasser then." He gave me a wicked grin. "Be careful though, he's not neutered."

My eyes went wide, and my mouth dropped open as Bob turned to walk down the stairs. "Wait, what's the dog's name?"

"Alpha." Bob turned to smirk.

That name brought back the memory of a cruel voice whispering in my ear. *'I'm the Alpha now, sweet thing. You're mine.'* Blood suddenly cold in my veins, I trembled with the memory of his hand, fisting my hair as he held my face down on the table. A sob choked out of my throat before I could stop it.

Frowning, all humor vanished from Bob's face as he stepped towards me. "Vera, what is it?" Shaking my head, I stumbled back to my room as the tears cascaded down my cheeks. "Vera?" The screen rattled as Bob tried to open the door, cursing when he found it locked. "Vera, was the man who hurt you called Alpha?"

Blubbering a quiet yes to my chest, Bob cursed again, then the place grew silent. Crying out the memories of the past fourteen years, I hugged myself, rocking back and forth. After a long time, I lay down exhausted and fell asleep.

Two nights later, I was sitting on my hammock reading when I heard a noise. Turning my head, I noticed the large dog sitting on the other side of the boundary. Easing myself out of the hammock, I went inside and filled a bowl with ice cold water, then a second bowl with the remainder of the stew I'd made for dinner.

During the week, the dog's appearance was sporadic but guaranteed every weekend. Taking it easy down the steps, I placed both bowls on the ground. Moving backwards up the steps, I lowered down to sit at the top stoop.

"I'm sorry I trespassed that first night I was here. I'd never been free to wander outside before, and it was too much to resist. Do you think we can be friends now?"

Tilting its head, the dog observed me. When it stayed where it was, I clasped my hands together and looked over the back yard. "It's beautiful here. I grew up in a house like the one up the hill. It was so big, a child should have been free to run and play, but my father yelled at me if I got underfoot." Taking a deep breath, I moved my eyes back to the dog. He'd come forward and was sitting by the bottom of the steps watching me as I talked.

"Bob told me your name. I'm trying not to hold it against you. My father held that title." Top of his nose scrunching as if he smelled something wrong, the dog stepped back. "No, he was a good man. He wasn't a great father, but he never hurt me. While he ruled the house, everyone ignored me. The chef basically raised me, and a teacher living in the house home-schooled me."

While I spoke, the dog came forward and sniffed my ankle. On instinct, I moved my leg away, and he sat back down to watch me.

"It was the man who held the title after my father that I hated. He didn't ignore me." Swiping at a stray tear running down my cheek, I hugged myself with my arms and shivered. Meeting the dog's eyes, he was intent on my tears. "Sorry, I'm rambling, aren't I? I'm not good at making friends. Freedom is still very new to me."

Rising up, I started back inside. As I shut the screen door, I looked back at the dog. "Try the stew. It was one of the chef's best recipes."

Locking the door, I turned off the inside lights and moved to my bedroom.

The next night, I cooked up the steaks Jeremy purchased me, insisting I needed the protein. Right on time, Alpha appeared in the yard. Serving up dinner on the plates, I walked out onto the patio.

When I'd collected the bowls later yesterday evening, all the stew was gone. The dog didn't stay by the boundary tonight. Last night I'd invited him to cross the boundary line, and he was taking that as an open invitation. Setting the plate on the bottom step, I went back to the porch and sat down with my meal. "Bon appetite."

Licking his steak for taste, Alpha rumbled then scoffed it down. Eating my half-portion, I smiled at Alpha, licking his chomps and eyeing my meal. Placing my plate aside as he came up the stairs, slowing as he approached me, I held my breath. Sniffing my ankle first, the one I twisted, Alpha made a weird noise, and I tensed. When he licked my ankle, I jumped a little then giggled. "It's okay, no long-term damage done."

Lifting his snout, Alpha licked where I'd cut my shin. Lowering my hand with caution, I slid my fingers into the silky hair on his head. Tremors passed through him from head to tail when I combed my fingers down the fur of his neck. My fingers sparked with static electricity, relaxing me. Exhaling hard at the sensation that passed up my arm, I bit my lip and moaned. The tingling vibrated through my chest, making me aware of my heart. Butterflies took flight in my stomach, my belly hollowed, and things tightened below.

Opening my eyes wide, I blinked at my body's reaction to his soft fur. Sniffing up my leg and along my bare thigh, Alpha shoved his nose between my legs where he took a deep whiff. Jumping up, I pushed his head away as I stepped back. "Oh my god! When Bob warned you weren't desexed, he wasn't joking."

Raising his head, I swear his eyes were laughing at me. When I went to collect my plate, Alpha shoved his nose into the crook of my neck and made a sound of appreciation. Confused, I tilted my head to look at him, and as I did, Alpha licked straight up the side of my face.

"Yuk! That's gross. It's bad enough when a man does it. Why do males always think it's okay to leak their bodily secretions all over a girl?" As I backed away, I swear Alpha raised a brow at me and laughed. Rolling my eyes, I walked back inside. "Now I need a second shower."

After showering and redressing in my pajamas, I came back out to collect the plates. A man was standing at the bottom of the steps. Halting my actions when I realized it wasn't Bob or Jeremy, I stepped back inside, locking the screen door.

Turning at the sound of the lock sliding into place, the man's deep indigo eyes watched me tremble. He was tall, with an athletic build, pale bronzed skin, dark hair, and the most luscious lips I'd ever seen on a man. He wore suit pants and a long-sleeved black business shirt, despite the summer heat outside.

It wasn't his looks I feared, but the air of authority he gave off. He held the composure of someone who got his way all the time. Not cockiness or ego, but the confidence you couldn't deny him whatever he wanted. Much the same as my father, and much the same as Malcolm. That's what made me shrink back from the door as he took the first step.

Collecting Alphas plate as he came up onto the patio, he held up a placating hand. "I'm not here to hurt you, Vera," his caramel voice assured.

Instantly, I felt at ease, but that set of its own set of alarms. Tears sprang to my eyes, my teeth gnawing on my lower lip.

"My name is Dale Hearn, I own the manor house."

Recognizing the name of the man who hadn't wanted me to own the cottage, I found it difficult to swallow. Was this about Bob and Jeremy?

Lifting the plate up before setting it down outside the back door, Dale cocked a brow. "You like dogs?"

Hugging my arms around me, stepping from foot to foot, wanting to run, hard and fast, and yet, I wanted to run to him.

His eye's assessing every movement I made. "It's about time we get to know each other, as neighbors, don't you think?"

"No." I nodded. Frowning, I forced my head to shake instead.

Jaw clenched, Dale slipped his hands in his pockets and watched me. "Bob told me someone hurt you before, that you're scared of our kind." With him watching me like a hawk, something about his eyes seemed familiar. "I give you every assurance, Vera, neither I or any of my staff will ever hurt you."

My heart warmed wanting to believe him, but my past etched distrust deep into my bones.

"I'd like you to come to my house for a dinner party tomorrow night. Bob and Jeremy and some friends will also attend, so you don't need to worry about being alone with a strange man."

The invitation sounded sincere, but I hesitated. Socializing and meeting new people and making friends appealed. Was I ready to risk this? "Will Alpha be there?"

Dale's eyebrows rose. "The dog?" When I nodded, Dale blinked a few times. "He'll be around, but I don't let him in the house."

"I'll come if Alpha will walk me home afterward."

"You trust the dog that attacked you over men that have done nothing but help you?"

Wondering how he included himself in that category, I frowned. "I trust the animal that has a truthful nature, over men whose nature is to deceive and manipulate."

"That's a wide net you are casting, Vera."

"It's a well-tested one."

Eyes scanning down my body, Dale paused his assessment at my waist. "That's a nasty scar. Care to tell me how you got that?"

Glancing down, I noticed that by hugging myself, my singlet had ridden up enough to flash the bottom part of the scar. Clearing my throat, I tugged the singlet down roughly. Dale's eyes jumped to my breasts in surprise. My cheeks burned when I realized I'd come close to exposing myself to him. Releasing the bottom of my singlet, I fitted it back into place, covering my chest. "Your dog trashed my dressing gown."

A smile curved Dale's lip. "You were trespassing; be grateful that was the only clothing he destroyed."

Gawping at Dale, I was astounded he could be so... who was I kidding, Malcolm would have said worse. Hell, he would have walked in here and stripped me down and...

"Bob told you?" Shivering at the near memory of Malcolm's persona.

Taking a deep breath, Dale rested a hand on each side of the door frame as he watched me. "My staff tell me everything that happens on my property."

"This isn't your land anymore."

He didn't debate with me, just smirked at the floor for a moment then lifted his eyes to mine again. "It's interesting."

"What is?"

"Bob and Jeremy both tell me you have brown eyes, but currently, they are a very vivid green."

Biting my lip, I touched a finger pad to my eyes.

"I'm guessing contacts. I'd place a decent bet that your hair wasn't mahogany till recently and that your real name isn't Vera."

"Get off my land."

Dale tilted his head. "I'm not threatening you, Vera. I'm just letting you know, I see past the charade." Stepping back from the door, Dale slid his hands into his pockets. "You're terrified, not of me or other men, just the one that gave you that scar. You've stood your ground against me several times now. I know you're a strong woman, you wouldn't be here now if you weren't."

Backing up another step, I swallowed the fear of his words, the awareness in his eyes.

"The accounts I've heard of you is that you are quite put together until a man goes to touch you." Dale's eyes drifted to my abdomen, hidden by my singlet now. "I would say that's warranted. So here's the deal, Vera. You're to come to dinner at my place tomorrow night. None of my guests will touch you, and Alpha will escort you home afterward. Hell, the entire pack can walk you back if that would make you feel safer."

Anxiety crawled along my spine. My father and Malcolm aways called their household by that term. "Pack?".

Sobering, Dale met my eyes. "There is more than one dog up at the house. Alpha was the one you had the misfortune of meeting when you arrived."

"Oh."

Studying me, contemplation evident on his face, Dale took a breath and refocused. "Dinner is at six. The dress will be smart casual." Turning on his heel, Dale walked back down the stairs without another word. Moving forward, I watched him move into the woods, following the lit path. He was so like Malcolm, and yet so different. Yes, he was an alpha male, but he reminded me more of my father on the brief times I saw him. My body felt safe around Dal. My muscles relaxed, and my heart calm. It was my personal trust issues, and the fact Dale seemed very familiar, but I couldn't put my finger on why.

CHAPTER 4

Opening the door to take a walk, I nearly had a heart attack to find a man standing there. "Jeremy?"

Without greeting, Jeremy moved past me and into my bedroom. "It's time I looked at your wardrobe."

"No, wait." Recovering from my surprise, I followed him into my bedroom. Already standing in the wardrobe, Jeremy frowned and moved to the dresser. Opening the empty drawers, he shook his head. Next, he lifted the pillow on my bed, noting my folded pajamas before entering the bathroom.

After assessing the near-empty clothes hamper, Jeremy came back out unhappy. "You own the clothes on your back, two other tops, and the pajamas under your pillow."

"I've not needed anything else."

"Can you not afford clothes?"

"Of course I can, I just haven't..." Swallowing, I hung my head. "There were so many people when I went to the shops. I've only just got used to the village, the shopping center was too much."

"Grab your purse." Walking out the front door again, Jeremy headed for his car. Unsure what was happening, I stared after him.

"Now, Vera. I have a dinner to prepare for so you'll have to shop while I shop."

Swallowing my hesitation, I grabbed my handbag and followed Jeremy out the door. He stood holding the passenger door on his Mercedes open. Hurrying forward, I sunk into the passenger seat.

Before starting the engine, Jeremy handed me a handkerchief. "Here, put it in your purse. You start to freak out, pretend to wipe your nose and breathe deeply; it will calm you."

"What's it laced with?"

"Don't ask. It will work, that's all that matters."

Shoving the hankie in my handbag, Jeremy pressed the ignition button and sped up the drive. Sped might have been an understatement. Jeremy drove like he was in a rally car tournament.

"Do you exercise?"

"I used to run on a treadmill every day. I've been walking around the house, but need joggers before I can run the driveway."

As if he guessed as much, Jeremy nodded. "There is a gym in the basement of the manor house. You play your cards right tonight, Dale will let you use it and the pool."

"What does playing my cards entail?"

Jeremy almost smirked; only almost. "No screaming, insulting, or gouging out the eyes of Dale's friends."

"I think I can manage that if everyone behaves themselves."

"They will." His voice was deep and confident.

When we arrived at the shopping center, Jeremy walked with me until I found a store that carried my style. After escorting me inside, Jeremy excused himself. "I need to go get some supplies. Go crazy, and don't hesitate to use the hankie if you need it."

When he started to reach for me, my eyes went wide, but Jeremy withdrew his hand. Grumbling under his breath, he walked out. Blinking at the awkward encounter, I started looking around the store.

Purchasing two summer dresses, a mid-season dress, some slacks, and loose flowing tops, I saw no sign of Jeremy. Spotting a sports store a few doors down, I made my way down to it. Staying close to the display windows, I held my breath whenever anyone came near me but made it unscathed.

With a pair of joggers and activewear in a bag, I hurried across the stream of shoppers to an underwear store. The underwear was stunning, but when I looked at the price tag, my eyes jumped out of my head. One set was more than I'd spent in total in the ladies sports store.

"Is there another underwear store here?"

The sales assistant smiled and considered the set I'd been admiring. "Yes, right at the other end. It's cheaper, but it won't feel or look as good. Why don't you try it first? You can then go to the other shop, and compare. What size are you?" Selecting one of the beautiful bras I'd been looking at, the sales assistant gestured me to follow. "Try it on, you'll notice the difference."

Hesitant, but keen to experience new things, I did as she said, and she was right. The lace was so soft and so well stitched that I felt naked in it. Turning to look in the mirror, the lace across my nipples was like a hot mouth passing over it.

Trembling in delight, I told the assistant I'd buy the set with the brief. She tried to convince me to go for the thong, but I declined. Malcolm liked g-strings, I preferred comfort. Since it was unlikely any man would see my underwear anytime soon, practicality was primary. Beautiful comfort was a bonus.

After trying a few more bras, I picked up a beautiful pair of summer pajamas in my size and handed it to the assistant. "What are those?" Pointing to an array of objects on a shelf.

"Have you never seen vibrators before?" The saleswoman asked. When I shook my head, she laughed. "Come on, honey, let's find something that will make you sing."

Showing me a few different items and lubricants, the assistant told me how to use them. By the time Jeremy walked in with his arms full of bags, my cheeks and chest were burning. He took one look at the girl holding the hot pink toy against my hand, went bright red, and stuttered he'd wait outside. That left the girl and me in fits of laughter.

After paying for my purchases, I walked out to where Jeremy was waiting. He cleared his throat. "Sorry, I took so long. I'm glad you were able to get to a few shops."

Gazing in the window at the stunning dressing gown hanging there, I sighed. It was full-length black satin with lace appliqué, and all lace from the knees down. Sexy but conservative.

"You like that?" Jeremy observed the dressing gown.

"Yes. But, that store cost more than all my other clothes together. That gown was twice that."

Studying the window with interest, Jeremy turned back to me. "You need anything else?"

"Dale said tonight was smart casual."

"Follow me." He led me to a boutique store. "Can I leave this here?" He asked the sales assistant as he put his groceries down. "I have to make a phone call." Pulling out his phone, he stepped outside, leaving me to browse.

Finding a lovely conservative tea dress, I tried it on. Sticking my head out of the changeroom, I saw Jeremy standing by the counter. Stepping out, I cleared my throat. Jeremy looked up and blinked. "Will this be okay?"

"Um," Jeremy coughed, "yeah, that works."

"Not one for compliments, are you?" The sales assistant rolled her eyes before turning back to me. "You look stunning, but you need heels." Before I could argue, she handed me a pair of black pumps in my size. Slipping them on, I had to admit, they made my legs look longer. Jeremy stood there, staring at me like the men in Malcolm's house used to do.

Unease spread through my body. Stepping out of the pumps, I hurried back into the dressing room. "What am I doing?" I asked my wide-eyed reflection.

"Everything okay?" The sales assistant asked.

Looking down at the dress, I felt the panic rising. I'd been intending to go unnoticed, to be dull, and not worth looking at. This dress didn't do that. It was the most conservative dress in the store, and it still drew attention to my feminine curves.

Unzipping the dress, I stepped out of it and pressed my back to the wall as breathing became difficult. Jeremy stepped into the change-room, reached into my purse, and retrieved the hankie. Before I could react to his presence, he put it in my hand, then to my face before pulling me against him and holding tight.

"Shh, it's okay. Breathe deep."

Holding the hankie to my face, I breathed in through my nose. The scent was masculine and heady. My knees went weak, and my head swam a little as Jeremy's hands rubbed up and down my bareback.

"Just relax. Nothing is going to harm you here." Waiting a few more minutes, Jeremy stepped back, removing his hands from me. "We good?"

Removing the hankie from my face, I nodded. "Yes, thank you."

Collecting the dress and shoes from the floor, Jeremy stepped out. Taking one last deep breath of the hankie, I shoved it away. That's when I noticed my clothes on the floor and realized I'd been standing in Jeremy's arms in only my underwear. Part of my brain was horrified and wanted to freak out. But the heady scent from the hankie was still circulating in my bloodstream; it kept me calm while I redressed.

Outside, I apologized to the sales assistant and left. Escorting me to the car in silence, Jeremy let the peace between us continue for the drive home.

"Do you have a bottle of that drug I could buy?"

"Like it did we?"

"It worked well. I don't think I could freak out right now if I tried. This is the most relaxed I've been since I was fourteen."

Sadness in his eyes, Jeremy observed me in a quick glance. "Do you know self-defense, Vera?" I shook my head. "It's about time you learned. You make nice with Dale tonight, then you'll come work out with me in the gym each morning I'm here. I'll teach you to defend yourself."

"In case Alpha jumps me again?"

Jeremy shook his head. "It will give you peace of mind. Give you the confidence you need."

Knowing if Malcolm ever found me, it wouldn't help me. Still, it could be handy for overcoming my fear of shopping centers.

Back home, Jeremy carried my bags inside for me, then told me where to come when I got to the main house for dinner. It wasn't till he'd left and I was putting away my purchases, that I found the extra bag with the tea dress and pumps.

Alpha was waiting by the back door for me when I came out. His tongue lolled out of his mouth, but it wasn't the only thing that came out. My eyes grew wide, and I shook my head. "We need to talk to Dale about getting you desexed."

Alpha growled at my suggestion, which made me chuckle. Doing the smart thing, I wore my flats trekking up to the house, carrying my pumps. Stalking beside me, Alpha's back came just above my hip level, making him the biggest dog I'd ever seen. Patting the fur on the back of his neck, I smiled at the electricity that sparked under my fingertips.

"So, you like my dress? You should see my underwear. It's the softest lace I've ever felt and all black." My fingers tingled with the guttural sound rumbling through Alphas body.

"I've decided I like black. It might be my favorite color, tone, whatever you want to call it." A breeze picked up, the promise of a summer storm blowing in. "I was never allowed to wear black. Malcolm liked me in white, liked to remember he took my innocence." Taking a breath, I calmed my disgust for the memory, but Alpha's presence chilled my hurt. "I've never had someone to talk to like this before. Thank you for becoming my friend."

Emerging from the forest path into the cleared backyard of the manor house, I got my first real look at it. The building was a three-story American style house.

There were a lot of large windows looking out over the back yard and the large pool area. Above the landscaped pool stood a large deck that spanned the entire back of the house.

Walking under the decking to reach the basement door, I worried when Alpha stepped in with me. "Are you allowed inside?"

Bumping my leg, Alpha turned off into what looked to be the gym. Alone, I left my flats at the back door and slipped on the pumps. With a sigh, I followed the directions Jeremy gave me until I

EBONY OLSON

found the steps which brought me up into the kitchen. There was a handful of waitstaff and cooks busy preparing who paid me no attention. Turning left, I found the living room. Jeremy and Bob were both there, along with three other men and five beautiful women.

Taking them all in, I wasn't worried about standing out and gaining men's attention any longer. With minimal makeup and my hair pulled back in a ponytail, I was unsubstantial next to these women.

Then there were the men. Bob and Jeremy, I already considered attractive, but the other three were handsome as all hell. Smart casual translated to Armani suits without a tie for the men, and cocktail dresses for the women. I felt like I'd stepped backstage at a fashion show.

"Vera, you look lovely," Jeremy greeted, coming towards me as if I might spook and bolt.

"I look like a cheap knock-off next to these people."

Tilting his head, Jeremy appraised the rest of the room. "You've bought a house with cash, Vera, there is nothing wrong with being conservative." He got a gleam in his eyes. "Are you wearing the underwear you purchased today?" My cheeks grew hot, and a smile teased the side of his mouth. "Then you've spent more on that then they have."

Studying the women, I frowned and returned my assessing gaze to Jeremy's wicked gleam. "They aren't wearing underwear, are they?"

Taking a drink of the beverage he was holding, Jeremy shrugged. "Just slows things down later." Waiting for the heat to fill my face and chest, Jeremy winked at me and turned back to the room. "I'd introduce you, but that's Dale's job. I'll get you a wine instead." His eyes went over my shoulder. "If that's okay with you?"

"Yes, thank you." As I turned to see what he was looking at, all I could see was a wall of black. Lifting my eyes from the black dress shirt and jacket, I discovered Dale. His hair was wet like he just stepped out of a shower, and his indigo eyes pierced me as they met mine. He was so very tall and so very close. My panties became damp,

28

and I wasn't sure if that was being turned on or wetting myself with fear.

"Evening, Vera. Thank you for coming. It's horrible to be the only stag at a dinner party." When Dale smiled my sex clenched, and I knew the dampness in my underwear wasn't weak bladder control.

Shaking his head humored and almost smiling, Jeremy went to the kitchen. Peering into my eyes, Dale frowned. "I prefer your natural color."

"I'd prefer to be unrecognizable. My eyes have always been my standout characteristic."

Lifting a brow, Dale let his eyes roam down my body and back again. "You have many standout qualities, Vera, your eyes are just my favorite."

Standing there mesmerized, I noticed the chocolate brown striations around his pupils. "Why are you so familiar to me?"

"Here you are," Jeremy interrupted, handing me a glass of wine.

"Thank you." Accepting the wine, I drank a mouthful.

Leaving us alone, Jeremy walked down into the room. Taking a glass of something a waiter handed him, Dale looked at me. "Vera, may I touch you? Just here." Placing his hand into the small of my back, he watched my face. Tensing on instinct, I cringed on the tightness that caused in my injuries and forced myself to allow it.

When Dale steadied his hand against me, my eyes fluttered with his touch. It was like he was running his fingers over my bare skin, eliciting a wanton reaction. His hand was still, but my skin was tingling under the thin material of the satin dress I wore. Beyond that, I felt safe with him. Moving closer to me, Dale lowered his mouth to my ear. "You're so warm."

"You're hot." Dale chuckled. Cheeks heating, I mentally kicked myself. "I meant your hand is hot."

"Will I introduce you?" Using his hand to walk me into the living space, Dale kept his body close to mine. Everyone turned to watch us like Dale's presence was magnetic. "This is Vera Cana, my new neighbor." He then proceeded to introduce me to everyone.

They were all very friendly and cordial. Some of the girls noticed

Dale's hand placement on my back, and nearness, but didn't seem phased by it. The men seemed to regard it more than the women.

Breathing deep, I let my senses take in the room. There was some flowery perfume on the women, but from the men, it was all musk and earth. Memories of the men from my childhood home intruded, how they all carried a similar scent.

The safety that Dale's presence usually provided vanished. Panic shot through my body and adrenaline injected into my bloodstream. This scene was all too familiar.

Trying to step back, Dale's hand felt like a restraint. Thankfully, I was well-practiced at controlling my reactions. Turning to meet Dale's eyes, I used the movement to remove his hand from me. Touching him made my fingers itch.

"Bathroom?"

Dale's smile was already gone, and I had no doubt he felt me tense up. Eyes flicking to a door by the kitchen, Dale shook his head and pointed in the opposite direction. "End of the hall, turn left, through the door, and it's on your right."

My entire body trembling, I tried to be casual walking out of the entertainment area. "Is that her?" One of the men asked someone else as I walked down the corridor. "She's not what I expected."

Once out of sight, I hurried around the corner. Opening the door, I stepped through, then shut it behind me as breathing became diffi-cult. The room was a large bedroom, king size bed, with masculine colors. I didn't have to guess whose it was, I could smell Dale all through this room. Expecting his scent to make my panic worse, I prepared for it. Instead, it calmed me. Taking deep breaths, I tried to be logical.

Running out of here screaming wasn't sensible. If I could keep it together for the next hour, then I could get through the evening, and go home. Then I'd distance myself from Dale and his household. That meant selling and finding a new place to live. Groaning, I moved into the bathroom. How did I escape one pack-house just to move in next door to another? What were the chances of that happening?

Tears started running down my face, unbidden. My body trembled with the need to cry with despair. "Is this because I touched you?" Dale asked from the bathroom door.

Lifting my eyes to meet his in the reflection, I sucked in a breath. "You promised you wouldn't."

"I never promised that. I said my guests wouldn't touch you." Dale's eyes traveled my body. "It would be impossible not to touch you. It is my natural instinct to do the exact opposite. I won't make a promise I can't deliver on."

Sucking in a shaking breath, I needed to know. "Is this a pack-house?"

CHAPTER 5

*S*tepping into the bathroom, Dale slid his hands into his suit pockets. He appeared contemplative. "We aren't like the packhouse you ran from, Vera. We treat women like the precious things they are."

My heart stuttered and fell in my chest as I closed my eyes. "You know where I came from?"

"Yes. There has been a lot of chatter amongst the packs about a woman almost killing Alpha Malcolm. A lot of speculation about the sort of woman who could do that. A full-blooded female of our kind."

Tears flooded from my eyes as I backed away from Dale. There was only one way out of this room, and Dale was blocking it. Trembling with adrenalin, I scouted for anything I could use to defend myself.

Not coming any closer, Dale shrugged. "Anyway, she died. Suffered a pulmonary embolism while recovering from her injuries in hospital."

My throat convulsed aware that Dale knew where I'd been in hospital. His lawyer had confronted me in my hospital bed. That had been far from here, and even further from Malcolm's pack-house. But

Malcolm had needed to treatment at the same hospital before I died there.

EYES full of intent as they met mine, Dale hypnotized me with his indigo gaze. "She's in a better place now. If she did what the rumor mill claims, then she earned her freedom. I'd never take that from her."

SURPRISING ME, Dale turned to leave, keeping his eyes on his bedroom. "I'm sure your life was hell, but I would like to help you get over that, Vera. As much as anyone could." Peering at me over his shoulder, his eyes sincere as he held out his hand to me. "See out this dinner with me; I'll allow Jeremy to train you."

Staring after him for a moment, I took a few breaths. My mind needed a moment to process how that encounter hadn't resulted in how I feared. My head spun, trying to accept that Dale hadn't hurt me or worse when he trapped me in this room. In fact, his retreat to his bedroom opened the path to the exit. It was as if he created that distance, understanding my anxiety.

Facing Dale with my entire body, I wiped my tears as best I could and indicated to my face. "I'll need a moment."

"I'll wait right out here."

Able to feel him out there, I closed my eyes and took several deep breaths. Turning back to the bathroom mirror, I cleaned my face up. Thank god, I hadn't bothered with foundation. "Are the women here part of your household?"

"Two of them are," Dale answered from further in the bedroom.

"Are they full-blooded?"

"No. Their mother was human."

Moving to the doorway, I found Dale by the end of his bed, watching me from the darkness of his room. "If they have children with one of the males, will that give you a full-blood?"

Eyes squinting, Dale shook his head. "Their children would then

33

have to mate with a full-blood." Moving forward, a frown creased his forehead. "Was this never explained to you?"

"I only know alpha meant the boss because of the way they used it."

"So you know nothing about your own heritage? Know nothing about why we are different?"

His wording got my attention. "Different how?"

Lightning flashed in Dale's eyes. Anger blew through the room like an unexpected hurricane. Scurrying out of the way, I squeezed myself between the freestanding bathtub and the wall. Hunkering down into the smallest possible size, my body quaked with fear. Memories of Malcolm stormed my mind, then blew away. No, it wasn't Malcolm; I had been right about Dale, he was different.

Malcolm's anger was choking, like a pair of nylons strangling you. Dale's rage left you unable to breathe, think, beg, or hope. Nothing but cowering, awaiting the hellfire of his wrath to tear your flesh and burn your bones to ashes. Like a neutron bomb, his temper sucked the oxygen from my lungs. Seconds later, the air returned to normal and rushed into my lungs, causing me even more pain than when it went. Wheezing, I panted for breath, curled over my knees, petrified.

"Vera." Dale rushed into the room, remorse coating his voice. "Oh, goddess, I'm so sorry." When he reached for me, I flinched. Hesitating only a moment, Dale proceeded to place a firm hand on my back and press down.

My eyes widened as my breathing hitched then immediately evened out. Calmness radiated through my body. The offering was safety, assurance, and love. Yanking back from that last emotion, I glared at Dale. He had the decency to wince. "Too far, too soon?"

"Too far."

Dale snickered. "Well, at least you recover fast." Rising up, Dale held out a hand. "Come on, Vera, dinner is ready."

Taking his hand to help me up, my nerve impulses fired where he touched my skin. Removing my hand from his, shaking still, I lifted my eyes to his. "You frightened me."

Something flittered across his eyes, but it wasn't an emotion I recognized to capture. "Can I show you something?" When I gave a slight nod, Dale gazed into my fake brown eyes. "I will need to touch you."

Pausing, I swallowed but decided there was nothing malicious in it. Cautious, but willing to give Dale the chance, I gave a single nod again.

Slipping his hand behind my neck, Dale pulled me close, my body pressing to his, as he brushed his lips against mine. Sighing at the feather-light touch, I stared up into his swirling indigo irises. The chocolate striations spread until only a ring of indigo remained on the edge of amber.

A growl of hunger rippled through me. Grabbing Dale's collar, I was hot and needy as I smashed my mouth against his, lips pinching and pulling. His gaze drew me in, and I fell; somewhat like I imagine Alice felt falling into wonderland.

Images of a woman in period wear, early nineteen hundred at a guess floated in my mind. She was walking down a cobblestone street with her mother. When the young woman noticed me watching her, she blushed. Her mother scowled and dragged her along faster.

In the forest, at night, the girl smiling as she stepped inside the tree line, dressed only in her nightdress. She didn't stay covered for long. Desire rippled through me as I watched the girl panting beneath me. Sweating and smiling, I loved the way she bit her lip as I lost myself inside her.

Her tears and fear as she told me she was with child. Stealing her away into the night, taking her from her family and making her my wife. Her belly heavy with child as I knelt and kissed it. Watching my beautiful twin girls born into the world.

Being happy, playing with my daughters, loving their mother, a lot. Considering the relentless practice, it took years for her to get with child again, but that was the way of our kind. Children were scarce. Still, I was over the moon to see her tummy grow a second time, followed by the birth of my son.

When I found her with another man, rage burned within me. Calm as a summer breeze, she touched my face and made me look in the mirror. Dale's youthful face reflected back at me. He looked eighteen at most. She made me see hers, no longer the young woman, but a matured one with teenage daughters.

As she explained that it was time for her to find a man of her own kind, to grow old in happiness, I seethed. With a farewell kiss to my lips, I let her go, wanting her happiness more than anything.

Dizzy, strong arms held me tight as Dale removed his lips from mine and I returned to his bathroom. "I cared deeply for Rebecca. When I found out about her affair, I felt betrayed. I'd never felt that much anger in my life."

Having felt his rage back then, it was ten times what I'd experienced in the bathroom.

"I could hold my temper when I felt gutted and betrayed by someone I cared about. So, I can hold my temper with anything you dish out."

Taking a second to find my voice, I licked my lips. "How did you do that? Are you a witch or something?"

"We have a connection that allows me to share my memories and experiences. You could share yours with me, but I don't think it's a good idea for us to dredge that lake. All you need to know right now is that connection will make it impossible that I will ever harm you, Vera. You are safer than Rebecca, and I could never have harmed a hair on her head, even when she broke my heart."

His lips were still only millimeters from mine. Tempting me. "I want to trust you. My instinct tells me too. The scars are still too fresh." Detaching myself from him, I created space between us, cold with the lack of contact.

Dale's eyes dropped to my covered abdomen. "Malcolm is a monster. I'm sure the scars are deeper than flesh, but I will help you heal what I can." Holding out his hand, palm up, Dale tilted his head to the door.

Sliding my hand into his, the tingles climbed like ivy along our connecting flesh. As we walked out to join the others for dinner, Dale chuckled to himself.

"What?"

"I can see in your eyes what your instincts are wanting right now. Most consider that dessert."

Heat flushing my entire body, I hid my face by looking at my feet, biting my lip? "Can you blame me after the porn show you showed me?" Looking around, I noticed the lounge area was now empty.

"They are already seated waiting for us." Placing his hand into the small curve of my back, Dale directed me into the dining room.

Did I let him touch me without flinching? 'Yes, you did.'

Sitting next to Dale at the long stone table, I studied the two girls who were spitting images of each other. Now that I'd seen her, I recognized their mother in them. The girls' flaxen hair, olive skin, and bone structure was their mother's. Their indigo eyes were their father's. They were stunning, there were no two ways about it. Considering I knew they were born over a hundred years ago, they looked around twenty-five.

Frowning, I wondered if the immortality was a magical thing. Malcolm and his household had never aged in the twenty-eight years I'd lived there. If living is what you could call it.

"I'm into men," Alexia, the twin opposite me, chirped as she lifted her wine glass to her lips.

Realizing I'd been staring, I cleared my throat. "I'm sure men are into you too."

Her sister, Hymn, giggled. "Are you into men, Vera?"

"I haven't had many options."

Everyone at the table stopped and stared at me. Clearing his throat, Dale placed his hand over mine on the table. "Vera has come out of a long term relationship not long ago."

It made me wonder what his household knew about me that he didn't mention who.

"How long were you together?" Juliet, who was sitting next to Bob, was pretty; model like beautiful. But she didn't have the earthy smell like Dale's daughters.

"Since I was fourteen."

"Oh, gosh, wow! So he's the only man you've ever been with? Why did you leave him?"

"Because I finally could." Picking up the wine in front of me, I took a mouthful.

When Juliet looked confused, Bob leaned into her, dropping his volume. "He used to beat her."

"Oh, God, how horrible." Ready to cry, Juliet gazed with sympathy at me. "Well, at least you are young. You can go out and live your life and have fun now."

"I'm twenty-eight."

"Really? You don't look old enough to have finished college. What face cream are you using?"

Beauty products brought Cindy and Heidi into the conversation with Juliet. Alexia and Hymn chuckled while the wait staff served the entrees. Taking his hand from mine, Dale started eating his salt and pepper squid. Missing his touch, I blinked and stared at my fingers.

"Are you settling into the cottage?" Adam, one of the Armani clad men, smiled, ignoring the girls' cosmetics debate.

"I am, thank you. Bob and Jeremy have been accommodating."

His eye's shifting to Dale and raising a brow in question, Adam chuckled and shook his head. "I'm glad to hear it. Do you work?"

Nodding as I chewed a piece of squid, I forced myself to swallow. "I'm a freelance graphic designer and web designer."

Brow lifting, Adam's eyes were molten warmth like a puppy dog. "You have formal qualifications?"

"No." Looking away, I took a gulp of wine.

"I meant no criticism, Vera. I was only wondering if you went to college?"

"No. I never left the house unless it was with him. I was home-schooled, and my teacher taught me web design so that I could assist the family business."

"If you worked for the family business, how'd you make money to buy the cottage?" Howard had the same rough manner as Jeremy and a physical resemblance. But unlike Jeremy, Howard didn't make me feel safe. In fact, out of all the men present, his gaze oozed over me like slime and made me shiver.

"I was working freelance for years, earning my own income."

Seeing Howard get ready to question further, I jumped in first. "What do you all do?"

Shifting beside me, Dale set his fork down to collect his glass. "I run a model and talent agency. Everyone at this table, except Jeremy and Bob, are one of my employees at the agency."

Peering around the table, I started chuckling.

"Something funny?" Howard asked unamused.

"The moment I walked in here, I felt like I'd gone backstage at a fashion show. Now, I know why. How come you and Bob don't model, Jeremy?"

Jeremy lifted a brow at me as if to ask if I was serious. "I have a business degree; I'm not selling my body."

"Hey!" Several voices complained around the table, especially the girl on his arm.

"I am Dale's personal assistant, not an eight pack."

"I thought you were the butler?" Everyone snickered at my question. Sniggering at the insult on Jeremy's face, Bob lowered his head.

"Jeremy is filling in until I find a new chef," Dale clarified.

"I'm the only person here who can cook a damn. That's why," Jeremy added snidely.

"A five star Michelin chef taught me to cook. Just ask Alpha, he's been enjoying my cooking for a month now."

Everyone looked to Dale who smirked but said nothing. Jeremy huffed into his drink, but the side of his lips tempted a smirk. "No wonder that mangy wolf has been off his food. He's getting fed elsewhere."

Alexia laughed. "Be careful, Vera, once you feed a dog, you can't get rid of them. We'll come home to find Alpha living down the cottage." Turning her gaze to Dale, she winked.

"Not likely. I'll move Vera in here before that ever happens."

Dropping my cutlery, I knocked my glass as I started shaking, but managed to catch it before it spilled. "Sorry." Taking a deep breath, I hid my hands in my lap.

Reaching behind me, Dale placed a hand at the back of my neck as he leaned in and lowered his voice. "Calm down, Vera. I didn't mean that like it sounded. I meant Alpha wouldn't be moving to the cottage, that's all."

As the main course came out, Dale pulled away and used his fingers to massage my neck until the plates were set down. The chatter continued throughout the main meal and dessert. They gossiped about colleagues, asked Dale for particular gigs, and other random stuff. No one asked me any more questions. Every time someone looked at me, Dale gave them a hard look, and they'd discuss something else.

When the meal finished, I excused myself to freshen up as everyone left the table. As I came back to the living area, there was raucous laughter. The models were making their way to the steps downstairs along with the other five males. "What's going on?"

"Time for a swim," Alexia giggled. "Come on, join us."

"Oh, I didn't bring a swimsuit."

"Neither did we." Juliet winked before disappearing down the stairs, leaving me alone with Dale.

Eyeing me as he handed me another glass of wine, Dale smirked. "Are you sure you don't want to join them?"

"I paid way too much for this underwear to destroy it in a pool."

Eyes sparkling, Dale opened the glass doors onto the decking and motioned me to follow. Taking a deep breath, I stepped out onto the dark decking with the most gorgeous guy I'd ever met.

CHAPTER 6

"*D*o they all live here?" Watching the pack of naked models dive into the pool below, I turned around and studied the house.

"They all have rooms here, but we all have our own places in the city. I'm home every weekend, or other days it suits me. We have a pack dinner once a month; otherwise, they come home when it suits them."

"Bob lives here?"

Dale turned his body to face mine. "He does."

"But not Jeremy?"

"During the week, Jeremy lives in the city. When he is here, Jeremy shares a room with his cousin. He was planning on taking the cottage. The house is large, but we have run out of space for the pack members. It's unusual for one of our kind to have many children. The girls share a room, but my son has his own."

"I could pick Hymn and Alexia as your daughters, which is your son?"

Shifting his weight, Dale pressed his lips into a firm line before speaking. "He's not here tonight, but you've met before. My lawyer who tracked you down at the hospital to demand you sell the cottage back to me."

Standing straight, I focused on trying to remember him. "That's why you look familiar. How did you find me?"

"Adam trained in computer forensics before joining the agency. Most of my pack have many qualifications, and they work for me when they want time out." Assessing me, Dale shifted his weight. "Why did you buy it? You hadn't even seen it."

"The picture just called to me. That nature surrounds it, and it came furnished was the clincher. It's hard to explain, but I knew it was where I needed to be."

Where we stood out on the decking Dale's indigo eyes appeared dark, but I saw them brighten at my words. Caressing my cheek, Dale gazed into my eyes. The swarm of butterflies lodging in my stomach since meeting him erupted. "You are exactly where you need to be." His voice was tight; almost a whisper.

Lost to his caress and eyes for a moment, I caught myself and pulled away, taking several steps to distance us. "I should call it a night. You may want to join your friends?"

Snickering, Dale raised a brow. "I don't know what it was like where you come from, Vera, but here, a father does not skinny dip with his daughters."

"Oh my god. I'm so sorry. I totally forgot and..."

Chuckling, Dale took both my shoulders in his hands. When I flinched but held my ground, Dale sobered. "I know you didn't mean to insult me, relax."

Moisture welled in my eyes, and I had to concentrate on my breathing to prevent the tears from falling.

"He would have hit you for something so innocent as that?" I nodded. Gritting his teeth, Dale took a deep breath. His anger pulsed in the air, but it was gone before I could acknowledge I'd felt it. "You said a professional chef taught you to cook?" Stepping back from me, Dale changed the subject.

"Y..yes."

Gesturing to his kitchen, Dale cocked a cheeky brow my way. "Care to whip us up an after-dinner snack?"

Eyeing his beautiful clean kitchen, I relaxed and followed Dale inside. "Anything particular you fancy?"

Eyes roaming my body, Dale smiled as he met mine. "Surprise me."

Giving him the biggest grin, I raided his fridge and pantry to find ingredients and see what I could make. Malcolm never let me choose. There was always a set menu or a specific request that I needed to serve. Never was the choice mine. The excitement was overwhelming. "Do you have a sweet tooth?"

"Very much so." Appraising my body again, Dale licked his lips. It wasn't creepy the way he did it. His gaze was a civilised gentleman with an edge of a tease.

Turning back around when the heat rushed to my cheeks and chest, I grabbed up what I needed and started mixing. Observing me, Dale sat with a smile on his face while I whipped cream and beat eggs in his kitchen. "Do you know you hum as you cook?"

Stopping long enough to consider he was right, I shrugged. "I like to have music playing when I cook. I love listening to music."

"You enjoy cooking for others?"

After placing the glasses of white chocolate and honeycomb mousse in the fridge, I cleaned up. "I do. Cooking was my first true love."

"Do you believe in true love, Vera?"

"Don't you? What about your ex-wife?"

"She wasn't my true love. I grew to care for her, yes, but had she not fallen pregnant, I would have ended it with her soon enough."

The happiness I'd felt cooking dropped out of my stomach, leaving me feeling hollow.

Reading my expression, Dale sighed. "I was young when I met Rebecca. I enjoyed seducing beautiful young women. I'd see them once or twice and then move on."

Turning my back, I kept cleaning so he couldn't see how unsettled I was by his admission.

"Rebecca changed that. I kept going back to her for weeks. She was different than the other girls, more confident. So, by the time I was ready to finish it, she was crying her news of being pregnant to me. I wouldn't abandon my children, so I married her, and I was a proper husband until she left me."

That surprised me, but not as much as when Dale turned me to face him and placed his strong hands on my waist to keep me near. "I was a cad. That stopped a century ago. Rebecca knew, Vera. She was rebellious and naughty to have ever laid beneath me, but she wasn't stupid. It's why Rebecca still sought the love of her life. She found him and died in his arms of old age, a grandmother to the children she bore for him. She was happy, and I could never deny her what she desired."

Studying his eyes, I found no anger or regret. "You hold no animosity towards her?"

"Why would I?"

This was so new to me. Didn't all men behave like suspicious, jealous, maniacs? Dale was so different. "I didn't think." Moving out of his hold, I dodged his approaching lips. "The mousse will need three hours to set. You'll have to enjoy them tomorrow night. I'm going to head home. Thank you for inviting me to dinner." Passive, Dale watched as I headed to the stairs. "Alpha?"

"Will be waiting for you. Head out, and he'll find you." Sliding his hands into his pockets, Dale relaxed with a sigh. He waited till I was standing on the first step downstairs to talk further. "Vera? Thank you for coming and giving me a chance."

Unable to resist giving him a semi-smile, I made my way down the stairs and towards the back door. As I changed my shoes, Alpha appeared beside me. Patting his head as we walked home, I kept my hand on his neck, enjoying the way stroking him made me feel light and free. Much the same way touching Dale did.

"Your owner is going to be a problem for me. I like him." Assessing the depth of that admission, I fell silent for a long moment. "I like him, but I don't trust him. Too many times before has charm, and false sincerity deceived me."

Alpha rubbed his head against my thigh in comfort. When we

reached my yard, Alpha stopped and let me approach the house alone. Bidding him farewell, I went inside and locked the door. Gazing back up the clear path towards the house, I collected my thoughts about the night. "I really like him."

STRONG HANDS CARESSED down my waist. A hungry mouth left a wet path down my midsection. Broad shoulders nestled between my thighs and scruff scratched across my tender folds.

"I'm going to devour you."

Biting my lip, I clutched my fist in Dale's thick dark hair. Fingers tingling with the contact.

"I'm going to make you cry my name until you can think of no other man but me."

My blood was burning up, my body aching for him to take me. When his tongue tasted me, it felt like he'd done so much more. My nerve responses fired like he'd electrocuted me. Arching my back, a cry of pleasure escaped my lips.

Growling, Dale lapped at my pleasure-center. Moaning, I squirmed beneath him, biting my lip to resist crying out his name until it mattered. A howl echoed through my room, startling me. Looking up, my eyes went wide at the big black dog standing over me, tongue hanging out in happiness.

"What the...?" Sitting up in bed, shocked, I looked around my room. It was dark, and I was alone. "A dream."

Sitting on the side of my bed, I scrubbed my face. I missed sex. The last fourteen years weren't always hell. When we were intimate was about the only time Malcolm was affectionate. He'd tell me how he loved me and adored me, and how good I made him feel. When you have no choice in the way your life is, you take the good days and make it count. So yes, I missed sex, because, for fourteen years, it was the only pleasure I'd known.

There was another howl, alerting me to what had intruded on my dream and woken me up. The full moon bathed the backyard in moonlight as I tiptoed through the dark cottage to the back door. It was beautiful. The lights to the manor house were out, and the gardens natural glow in the night was magnificent.

Unlocking the back door, I stepped out onto the back deck. The wind picked up and was a little chilly, but it didn't detract from the magical aura of the night. The energy of the night buzzed through me, calling me to run through the woods and revel in the goddess's light. Staying on the back patio, I watched the clouds blowing low and heavy through the night sky. At intermittent times, the clouds would block out the moon, and darkness would descend. It was only brief, and when the moon came back, it was worth waiting for.

Another howl close enough to be right next to me made me jump. Alpha stood inside the trees of the boundary line baying to the moon as if she was his long lost love. It left me awestruck. When he finished his moon song, he lowered his head and looked straight at me. Happiness flooded me that he allowed me to witness what seemed an intimate moment with him and the moon.

Clouds blew over again, darkness descended, and shadows slipped through the trees. Fear trickled down my spine. It was ridiculous. I knew it was the other dogs from the house, but still, there was something dangerous in the way they moved. Like ghosts chasing their salvation.

When a stag bounded into my backyard, I stood awed by such a magnificent creature. Then five large dogs descended on it. Stalking forward, the dogs surrounded the stag, and I knew they meant to kill it. The stag, brave even in the face of defeat, lowered its head and prepared to fight.

"No, don't!" Stepping forward as if I could stop the slaughter, I caught the dogs' attention. Stupid, I know. No one ever said I was a genius.

All the animals turned at my intrusion. Recovering first, the stag tried to use it to his advantage by rushing the dog in front of him. Realizing in time, the dog shifted but yelped as one of the stag's antlers collected his back leg and flipped him.

Three of the other dogs charged. One dog took the stag's throat while the others brought it to the ground. Covering my mouth in horror, I averted my gaze from the slaughter. Turning to rush back inside, I stopped wide-eyed and backstepped.

The fifth dog was on my porch, head, and body low, ready to pounce as it stalked towards me. Whimpering, I backed up. Weighting his paws, the dog who looked more like a wolf at this moment, readied to pounce. Trying to protect myself with my hands as he leaped, I closed my eyes and prayed to the goddess.

A crash and snarls rippled through the night, like a boulder thrown in the pond. Alpha held my would-be-attacker on the ground. Saliva dripping from his angry jowls as he threatened the other wolf. Because now that I'd seen them hunt, I recognized the breed. Not waiting to see more, I jumped the railing into the backyard, ran around to the steps, and raced up them. Bolting into the house, I slammed the door shut, jamming the locks in place before backing away from the door.

Trembling and hyperventilating, I was more scared than I'd ever been. Lighting flashed; I jumped. Thunder roared, and, as the rain started pouring, my legs turned to jelly. Falling to the floor, a heap of a spineless, blubbering, messed-up woman, I screamed. The lightning exposing me for the pathetic female I was. "I just wanted a safe, quiet place."

Another loud snarl followed by a dog's whimper before the thunder shook the cottage. "I just wanted to be safe."

CHAPTER 7

*T*aking a deep breath, I rang the doorbell. All morning, I'd made myself wait. Avoiding looking out to the ruins of the stag outside, I forced myself to try and eat breakfast - I couldn't. After dressing in my running gear, I ran my driveway and theirs to get to the front door of the manor house.

When the front door opened, Howard scowled down at me. "What do you want?" The way he looked at me was as if I were dog shit he'd discovered on the bottom of his expensive shoes. Blinking at the aggression of his greeting, I wondered how I offended him. Taking a careful step back out of arms reach, I bit my lip reconsidering coming here.

"Howard, don't talk to her like that." Coming to the door, Bob opened it wide and looked me over. "Vera, everything okay?"

Shaking my head, I assessed the two men. They both looked like they didn't sleep last night. "Your wolves chased a deer onto my property last night."

"Your property?" Howard growled stepping towards me.

Grabbing his shoulder, Bob hauled Howard back three steps, glaring at him but not saying a word.

Licking my lips, I nodded. "They came into my yard and surrounded the deer. I panicked and interfered, and one of your animals got hurt."

Eyes shadowed, Bob looked tired. "We know."

"I'm so sorry. I just couldn't stand to see the deer hurt. It was stupid, I know, I just wanted to make sure it was okay."

"The deer is dead you dumb-"

Grabbing Howard by his shirt, Bob shoved him back inside. "Shut it and piss off, Howard."

Feeling lower than a dog turd now, I shrank back as I cleared up the confusion. "I meant the wolf. I wanted to make sure your pet was okay."

Bob sighed; I'd never seen him unsmiling. "He's fine, Vera. He needed a few stitches, that's all."

Tears building, I nodded. All night, I'd been tossing around a decision, but Howard just made up my mind for me. "Is Dale here?"

Peering over his shoulder as if checking the coast was clear, Bob returned his eyes to me. "He's with the dog and the vet. I'll get him to walk down to see you later."

"No, it's fine. Can you let him know I'll cover the vet bill?"

"That's generous, but not necessary."

"And let Dale know the cottage is his. I'll sell it to him for the price I paid, plus transfer costs." Having made my decision, I turned to leave.

"Wait, what?" Stepping forward, Bob caught my shoulder. When I flinched away, he removed his hand while I put space between us.

"I came here for peace, not to watch animals get slaughtered, or for wolves to attack me every time I walk out my back door." Fourteen years of training to never raise your voice or talk back sticks like glue. "I came here to get away from a pack-house, not to end up in a new one. Dale can have the cottage." Jogging down the stairs, I ran towards the driveway.

"Shit!" Bob cursed behind me.

Back home, I showered before sitting down to look for a new

place. Since I was now used to the local area, I looked for a small place closer to town. Picking a few worth looking at, I phoned to make appointments to see them. One had an open house this morning, so I grabbed my keys and left.

When I arrived at the open house, Danny Ready was out the front with his ever-ready smile. "Ms. Cana, are you looking for an investment property?"

Groaning to myself that I'd put on a summer dress this morning, and now his eyes were all over my legs. "No, a place for me. The cottage isn't working out with the neighbors." Without any further explanation, I stepped by him. The house was a little two-bedroom home on the outskirts of the village.

The place wasn't as lovely. The neighbors were only spitting distance away, and it would need several renovations. Exhaling, I made my way back outside. Danny was on his phone when I came out. Hanging up when he saw me come back out, Danny moved into my path, his usual smile gone. "What did you think?"

"Not for me. Do you have anything else in this price range?"

Danny shrugged all apologetic. "Afraid not."

"What about the Hudson road place? I phoned your office and made an appointment to see it tomorrow?"

Danny rubbed the back of his head. Tilting my face to observe him better when his gestures reminded me of Bob. "Well, yes, they are in the price range, but even worse than this place."

Inhaling to hold my annoyance, I caught a whiff of a familiar scent. Beneath Danny's cologne earth and musk hit me. "I see." Anger started to bubble inside me. "Well, I'll take a look for myself. Goodbye, Mr. Ready."

In my car, I phoned the real estate. "Yes, Ms. Cana, we can confirm your appointment tomorrow."

"Excellent, Jessica. Do you have a female agent who can show me through?"

"Ah, yes we do, but Mr. Ready is the property manager."

"Jessica, is there any chance someone else could show me through? I'm still recovering from a rather violent domestic violence relationship. I don't feel comfortable being alone with a man?" Never did I dream I'd play the hell of my past to my advantage.

"Oh, of course. Let me check LeeAnn's diary. That shouldn't be a problem. Can I call you back to confirm a time?"

"That will be fine, thank you, Jessica." Hanging up, I exhaled letting my head thump back against my headrest. My eyes tracked to where Danny was standing out the front of the house. His eyes kept glancing at my car every couple of seconds. Maybe staying local wasn't going to work? The pack was bigger than I thought if at least two members missed dinner last night. Frowning, I realized that the two members not there were those involved in the house sale debacle.

Danny hadn't been the sale realtor, but that's who had the keys for hand over. Picking up my phone again, I searched google and hit the call button. "Hi, I'm after a locksmith..."

FINISHING DINNER, I was sitting on the back step with a glass of wine when Dale came down the path from the manor house. Climbing the steps, he sat next to me without asking. "The dog will be fine. It needed a few stitches, but don't worry about the vet costs. It should never have happened. You have my word; it won't happen again."

"The stag is the least of the problem, Dale." Cupping the wine glass in my hands, I stared into the red depths of it. "That's the second time one of your wolves attacked me. And who the hell keeps wolves as pets?"

Considering the wine glass, Dale cleared his throat. "To be fair, the first time you were trespassing. Last night you were responsible for his packmate getting injured."

"What's Howard's issue with me?"

Tensing, Dale blinked. "Why do you...?"

"He was mean to me this morning and looked at me like I was nothing. At least when Malcolm looked at me like that, I knew it was because I couldn't get pregnant. By failing to conceive, I made

Malcolm look weak. But Howard, he doesn't know me, so he has no right to look at me like that."

Dale's anger washed over me, stealing my breath from my lungs. Getting up, Dale walked away, putting space between us. "I didn't know he abused you. It won't happen again."

Taking a mouthful of the wine, I stood. "I know it won't. The cottage is yours. I just need enough time to find somewhere else."

"I don't want it anymore. I want you here. You'll be safe here."

"I'm not safe here, that's the problem. I'll sell it to you for what I paid."

Shaking his head, Dale slid his hands into his trouser pockets. "No. I'm not buying it off you."

"Fine, I'll list it on the open market tomorrow. I was giving you first option." Collecting my stuff, I stormed inside. The door opened behind me. Spinning around, my heart hammered in my chest when Dale came inside. "What do you think you are doing? Get out!" Moving to the sink, I put my dish and glass down, placing the bench between us.

"I won't let you sell it. You can't have saved enough money to buy another place, so you'll be stuck here."

Aghast, I turned to face him fully. "Why? You wanted this place enough three months ago that you had your lawyer come to my hospital bed to bully me into getting it back. What has changed so drastically in the past three months?"

"I met you!" Taking a deep breath, Dale calmed and met my eyes. "When I'm with you, something that I've never felt with any other fills me up inside. Like an emptiness, I didn't even know was there until we met. We need to explore that. I want to get to know you. And by the goddess, I want to bury myself so deep inside of you, no other man will ever reach that place within you again."

"Sex?" I glared at him. "You won't let me sell because you want to have fuck me? Fine, let's have sex. You can screw me all night long, get it out of your system, and then buy the cottage tomorrow."

Exhaling, Dale shook his head and shoved his hands in his suit pockets. "No." He lifted his eyes to mine. "You're not selling. You are safe here, and you'll stay here."

My anger burst open. "You're not my alpha! I'm not part of your pack-house, and you can't tell me what to do!"

Dale ground his teeth. "You are a female of our kind. Do you know how rare it is to get full-blooded females? There are two, in this entire country that anyone knows about, and I only know about you because I've met you. Your father hid you instead of celebrating you, and you suffered because of it.

"You missed the introduction. At age sixteen, your alpha should have arranged for you to visit other packs. Introduced to every single one of us until you met your mate." The wave of Dale's anger reducing the oxygen levels made me retreat. "That's protocol. Even with your father ousted, had we known about you, we would have forced Malcolm to protocol. We would have protected you, just on the off chance one of us was your mate."

Meeting my eyes, Dale tensed his jaw, a small cracking sound, and then he shook his head and took a deep breath. The indigo blue of his irises forced out as the chocolate brown striations engorged. As the brown took over, gold bloomed around his pupils and spread. Recognizing those eyes, I didn't understand how it was possible for them to be in a human face.

"I am filthy at your father because I've lost twelve years with you. I can't follow tradition with you because you don't even know what it is. I'm mad as hell at Malcolm because I have to walk on eggshells just to be near you. You won't acknowledge me, and you won't listen to your instincts about me because of what he did to you."

Staring, I couldn't even comprehend what he was on about anymore. My mind kept seeing a big black wolf with the same eyes as the ones Dale had right now.

"So no, you can't sell. No, I won't let you just disappear from my life now that I've found you, and no, I won't fuck you to get you out of my system. That will never happen." Storming out the door, he backtracked and turned around to growl at me through the screen door. "If you list this house for sale, I will make it impossible for you to sell. I will tie you up in so much red tape that the lawyer's fees alone will drain whatever resources you have left." Swinging around, Dale marched down the steps.

Left standing in my kitchen gobsmacked, it took me over two minutes after he went to react.

"How can you be him?"

CHAPTER 8

Still in my pajamas, I barely had my eyes open when the knocking at the front door started. Grumbling, I made my way to the door and opened it enough to see who was out there. The sight of Dale's lawyer son on my doorstep almost made me hiss. Dressed in his Armani suit, Cameron Hearn looked way too spritely for six on a Monday morning.

"Ms. Cana, good morning. I hope I didn't wake you?"

"Would you care?"

"I'm due in the office by nine, so I thought it best to get this out of the way early." Cameron Hearn handed me an envelope.

"Should I even ask?"

"We are filing an injunction preventing the sale of this property. As you'll remember from the conveyance report on your sale, you have no direct road access."

"What? I do so have road access."

"Actually, your driveway starts twenty meters up Mr. Hearn's driveway. That means every time you leave or enter your property, you are trespassing." Cameron handed me another piece of paper. "Formal notice that access via Mr. Hearn's driveway will cease until you can settle the matter." Cameron turned to walk to his car.

"Wait? Your father is trapping me here? How am I meant to go to my doctor appointments? Go food shopping? Anything?"

"Jeremy will continue to shop for you, as usual. The rest, I'm afraid, is your problem. You should have looked at your conveyance report better when you purchased, Ms. Cana."

Climbing into his expensive car, Cameron Hearn drove away. Angry as hell and in need of coffee, I made my way back to the kitchen. Setting the coffee machine on, I opened the documents and read the injunction. "Son of a bitch."

To fix the issue, I had to extend my driveway out to the road and have my own access. Since Dale owned the property surrounding mine, I had to buy the land from him to get to the street. To do that he was asking an exorbitant amount; almost what I paid for the cottage. Then I would need to pay for the fencing of his land and construction of a driveway to the road.

Considering I didn't have enough in my 'fuck off fund' to buy the land, building a driveway wasn't an option either. Being self-employed, a loan wasn't an option. Especially if they did a half-decent records check and realized Vera Cana was an alias. Frustrated, I picked up my coffee mug and threw it as hard as I could. The smash that followed cooled my temper for a second. When my eyes found the broken kitchen window, I swore like a drunken sailor.

Without driveway access, I couldn't even get a glazier to come and fix the window. Picking up a few more items, I threw them at the window, smashing the remaining shards still in the frame. The damage was done, I may as well work my anger out and make it easier to clean.

Three hours later, I'd knocked the remaining shards free from the frame and swept up the glass. The missing glass exposed the house to the elements, so I was grateful it was summer. At least it kept me busy until I could call my lawyer.

"I'm sorry, Vera, you don't have a legal footing here. They've allowed for you to still receive groceries and such. This is very well written."

"Can I at least leave? They can't trap me here, right?"

"If you cross his land without permission, he could have you arrested. For any other client, I would call the police and have them escort you from the premises. But, in your situation, you don't want the police involved and take the chance of them running your name. My suggestion? I would ring your neighbor and negotiate your way out of this dispute. He must want something to go to this effort. Maybe he doesn't want to pay full-price for the house. You may need to sell it to him at a loss."

Goddess, if that were even the reason. Hanging up even more annoyed, I hung my head but refused to cry. Leaving everything there, I changed into my workout gear and ran to the top of the driveway. Scouting my chances of making it to the road before Dale could catch me. It wasn't like the driveway was near his house. Unfortunately, I discovered a large padlock on the closed gate. Considering I'd never seen the gate closed, I wondered if they'd had to oil the hinges to swing it. Still, I could take a bag and jump the fence to make the road.

As I neared the gate, an animal prowled into view. It growled at me the moment it saw me. Studying the animal, I recognized straight away it wasn't Alpha and ground my teeth. It was the wolf that tried to take my throat out for interfering in their hunt.

"Oh, shut up! You know, I haven't finished going through the cottage yet, but if I find a gun, I'm going to come back up here and shoot you. Unlike the rest of your pack, you deserve putting down like any other dog willing to attack a human."

He started snarling and snapping at me through the gate. Giving it the finger, I ran back down the driveway. In my kitchen, I spied the broken window and groaned. There was now a huge gaping hole in my security. Deciding to be a woman of my word, I started searching the cottage for a gun or any other weapon. The best I found was a baseball bat.

"Something's better than nothing." Shrugging, I took it into the kitchen with me. For a moment, I considered having some batting practice with the remaining window. The look on Dale's face when he came down to gloat and found the place smashed up was almost worth it. That was after he got over the pile of shattered glass I left at the forest path to the manor.

After canceling my inspection appointments, I called my lawyer back to ask a few more things. With nothing much else I could do, I opened my laptop and did my work.

The knock at the front door on Wednesday occurred like clockwork. Cracking it open, I noted Jeremy laden with shopping bags and opened the door wide for him. Without saying anything, I turned and walked back down the hall and took my seat at my laptop.

"What the hell happened here?!" Jeremy moved from the kitchen bench to inspect the broken window.

Ignoring him, I kept doing my work.

"Vera?" When I still refused to answer, Jeremy stormed over to the table and slammed the laptop shut. "Answer me, damn it! What happened to the window?"

Glaring at him, I stood up and started walking away.

"Hey, I didn't do this."

"You didn't stop him either. Trapping me here is no better than what Malcolm did to me."

"That's bullshit! No one is beating you to a pulp."

Tears swimming in my eyes, I turned to face him. "Yet! This is how it starts, Jeremy. It's just a matter of time before I'm cowering every time he walks in the room. Do you even know what it's like? To have to be mindful of everything I say and do. How would you feel if while doing calculations in your head, you looked at him the wrong way? What if every perceived slight ended with you spending the night on the floor coughing up blood?"

"Dale would never hurt you like that."

"I don't trust you! I don't know any of you. Why would I choose to believe a word out of your mouth?"

"Get to know us!"

"Get out of my house, and from now on leave the groceries on the doorstep. None of you are welcome here anymore."

"Vera..."

"And tell your alpha, he may win this, but he lost me." Seething, I slammed my bedroom door shut in Jeremy's face. Sitting on my bed, I waited for Jeremy to leave, then I broke down and cried.

SEVERAL HOURS LATER, the sound of glass tinkling on metal disturbed my focus on my work. Rising from my table, I looked out the back to see Bob collecting the broken shards of glass into a wheelbarrow. Glancing to the house, he saw me and paused to wave. Turning away without acknowledgment, I went back to my work.

After finishing the lawn, Bob came to the back door and knocked. "Do you want me to do something about that window?"

"Can you ask your boss if he'll allow glaziers down to fix it?"

"I'll call him now." Walking away from the door, Bob took out his phone. It took fifteen minutes for him to come back. "We've called some guys; they'll be here in an hour to fix it."

Getting to my feet, I went to the kitchen and poured a large glass of water before taking it to the door. Unlocking it, I handed it to Bob. "Thank you."

Giving me a kind smile, Bob took the glass of water. "This shouldn't be happening. He should just tell you what you should have always known and then explain the protocol."

"You tell me." Crossing my arms, I leaned on the door. Looking like a rabbit in headlights, Bob fumbled for words. "Okay, let me ask a question. You guys are immortal, right?"

Eyes tight, Bob pressed his lips together before answering. A pulse of his frustration hitting me like a slap. "No, just very long lives."

Ignoring the sting of his mild temper, I focused on getting some answers. "And you can change into wolves, right?"

Throat convulsing on his next swallow, Bob nodded.

Trying not to react, I was hoping I'd imagined things the other night. "So, you're like werewolves?" Goddess, it sounded insane even to my own ears. If I were wrong, maybe Dale would think I was crazy and let me go.

"Lycans. We are our own species, born this way. Getting bitten by us doesn't turn you into one."

"But you breed with humans?"

"Human females, yes. Though, getting women pregnant is difficult." Avoiding looking at me, Bob dropped his head as if he were delivering bad news. "Our women are usually sterile. The closer to full-blooded they are, the harder it is for them to get pregnant and stay pregnant."

Pain bloomed in my chest from the impact of his words. "This is common knowledge in all the pack-houses?" My voice was weak, choked on my emotional pain.

Bob's eyes filled with sympathy. "Yes."

The only reason I didn't collapse in a heap on the deck was that Bob caught my shoulders. "So, every time they beat me telling me I was a failure, they knew that it was never going to happen?"

Voice tight as if he felt my pain, Bob held me to his chest. "Yes. It was just an excuse."

For a minute, I sobbed in his arms. Then trying to regain my composure, I squeezed my eyes to hold the tears and moved him away. Giving me space, Bob looked severe; caught between rage and overwhelming sadness.

"So, Howard is the one at the gate?"

"Yes."

"And alpha is Dale?"

"Yes."

Cringing on that one, I closed my eyes. I'd opened up to Alpha thinking he was a dog. Voice weak, I struggled to ask the next question. "Who did the stag hurt?"

Bob exhaled hard. "Jeremy. He and Howard are cousins, it's why Howard went for you."

Shaking my head, I refused to accept anyone defending Howard's hatred towards me. "No, it was just an excuse. You see, I know Howard's type, I lived in a house full of them."

"No one will harm you here, Vera. Dale won't allow it, and as his mate, he'd never harm you."

My eyes swelled with fresh tears. "I don't even know what that means."

"It means the goddess matched the two of you from your birth. Before your conception, fate designed you for each other. It means he will protect you and love you and never let anyone hurt you like Malcolm did again."

There was too much passion in his voice. His utter belief that his words were valid broke my heart because I couldn't believe them. Looking up into Bob's eyes, I needed a way to make him doubt as much as I did, or he'd convince me he was right. Then if I dared to hope and Bob was wrong, Dale would break my soul. I couldn't go through that again. "Are you neutered like you claimed?"

Bob's blue eyes lit up. "When it comes to you, yes. For every other woman, no." Sweeping my hair away from my face, Bob smiled down at me. "I said that, so you'd let me take care of you."

"I don't believe you." Going on tiptoe, I kissed him.

Bob froze for a second, then he pulled away. "That's not a good idea, Vera." Bob's eyes wide with surprise. "I'll finish my job."

Lunging forward, I kissed Bob again. Wrapping his hands around my waist, Bob groaned. Pressing against him, I rubbed my body all over his. Neutered my ass. Pushing me up against the door frame, Bob used his knee to spread my thighs and grind against me. His mouth hungry against mine, Bob growled and gripped me harder.

Smiling when his mouth nibbled down my throat, I knew I had him. Dale would come tonight, either as himself or Alpha, and he'd be able to smell Bob all over me.

Shoving away from me, Bob all but ran down the steps before he looked at me again. His face a mask of guilt and regret. "I'm sorry, Vera, you're not for me."

"Who says? Shouldn't it be my say who I have sex with?"

Mouth hanging open, Bob looked me over, his pupils dilating. "You want to have sex with me?"

"Did I not make that obvious?"

Jaw working as if he chewed gum, Bob's brows lifted. "But Dale is your mate, and he's the Alpha. With him interested in you, you shouldn't even notice another man."

"Maybe we aren't mates then?"

Bob was five seconds away from climbing back up those steps and screwing me here on the back patio. It was clearer than the sky on a cloudless day. When a mobile phone started ringing, we both kind of jumped. Tensing, Bob took his phone out of his pocket, staring at it as if Dale could reach through the screen and punch him. When he exhaled in relief and put it to his ear, I frowned.

"Good, no I'm fine. Can you bring them down? I've got to run into town." Putting more distance between us, Bob hung up and avoided looking at me. "The glaziers are here. Jeremy will bring them down. I need to go." He walked away before I could protest.

Kicking the door with the back of my heel, I forgot I was barefoot. Cursing when it stung, I limped back inside. I was so damn close. An alpha male would hate for a female he wanted to choose a lesser man. It was the perfect way to piss Dale off enough that he might let me leave. So damn close.

CHAPTER 9

*J*eremy wouldn't let the glaziers come in the house, he made them walk around, and he stayed clear of the door. Taking my stuff into my bedroom, I continued working in there. An hour later, there was a knock on the door. Huffing, I closed my computer and inched the door open to Jeremy's handsome face.

"Can we talk?"

"Just give me the bill, please."

"We've got it."

"Okay." Not even arguing with them about paying for the window repair, I went to shut the door.

"Damn it." Shoving his foot in the door, Jeremy pushed it open, forcing his way inside, then slamming the door behind him. "Enough!"

Whimpering, I backed away. What on earth made me think a place with no neighbors was a good idea? No one could hear me scream here.

"Goddess, I'm not going to hurt you, Vera, so can you stop cowering?"

Shuffling further back, I shook my head.

"Call him and tell him you'll stay. End this nonsense."

EBONY OLSON

Backing into my bedroom, I moved to try and shut the door. Stopping it with ease, Jeremy forced it open. Grabbing me, he set me against the wall. Tucking up in his hold, I covered the sensitive targets of face, neck, and abdomen by curling on myself.

"Vera." Voice soft, Jeremy tucked my hair behind my ear as he breathed over my head, followed by a long inhale. "Vera. Take a breath and look at me?"

Sobbing, I shook my head. That's how they open you up. They use soft words and feign sincerity. You let your guard down for a minute, lift your eyes, and they punch you in the face or grab you by the neck. I didn't beg. I learned long ago that begging makes it worse. It either urges them on or annoys them more. Either way, the result was more pain for me.

Pressing his body forward, Jeremy slid his arms around me and cuddled me, rubbing my back as he soothed me. "I hate seeing you unhappy and scared. I know you could be happy here if you gave it a real chance. If you gave us a real chance."

Hiccupping between sobs, I gasped for breath to respond. "Is that what you wanted to say?"

"It will do for now."

Pushing against his chest, I removed him from me. "Can you please leave?"

With a huff, Jeremy stepped back and turned to leave.

"Jeremy," he looked back at me, "I'm sorry I got you hurt."

Frowning, Jeremy tilted his head, then his brows lifted. "You know?"

Hugging myself, I slid down the wall.

"Vera, it wasn't your fault." Crouching down in front of me, Jeremy patted my hair as he soothed. "The guys shouldn't have chased the buck here."

"You still got hurt because of me." I felt so guilty.

"So, make it up to me. Stay."

Lifting my red-rimmed eyes, a spark of anger flashed in my chest. "I don't get a choice in that, do I?"

Lowering his head in defeat, Jeremy exhaled roughly. "We would

64

all do anything to keep our mate once we found her, Vera. A love like that is a once in a lifetime thing."

"I don't know what love is."

"Then stay and find out." Peering at me from below his heavy brows, Jeremy stood. Caressing my head, he left.

Checking the time on the clock, I crawled to my bed to get my phone. "Vera?" my lawyer answered the call once her secretary put me through.

"Make the deal."

"Vera, are you okay?"

The sob came unbidden, and before I knew it, I was crying outright.

"I can call the police?"

The police and the monster they could bring back into my life were the last things I needed. "No. Just make the deal."

"I'll call his lawyer now."

Thirty minutes later, Melissa emailed me to let me know they'd accepted my terms. Dragging myself into the shower, I dressed for bed, then curled under my blanket with Netflix.

Dosing when I heard the knock at the back door, I considered getting up to answer it. Changing my mind, I closed my eyes. An emotional wreck after the day, the last thing I wanted to do was talk to Dale. Instead, I drifted off to a place where men didn't control me, beat me, or hurt me while claiming to love me.

STRONG HANDS CARESSED *down my body. A hungry mouth created a wet path down my midsection. Then Dale's afternoon shadow scratched across my tender folds.*

"I've wanted you from the moment we met."

Biting my lip, I clutched my fingers in Dale's thick dark hair. My hands tingling with the contact.

"I'm going to make you cry my name so you will think of no other man but me."

My temperature was rising, my body aching for him. A lash of his tongue, I cried for mercy. Growling, Dale lapped at my heat. Moaning, I squirmed beneath him, biting my lip to resist crying out his name until it mattered.

A growl echoed through my room, startling me. Opening my eyes expecting Alpha, I shrieked to find Malcolm standing over me. His eyes were angry, his hands busy winding his belt around his fist, so the buckle hung down.

"Did you think I wouldn't find out you were still alive, Viridia?"

Whimpering, I shuffled up against the bed head as he shook his head.

"Dreaming of another man? First, you try to kill me, then you betray me."

"Malcolm..."

"I loved you, and you attacked me!" Raising his arm, Malcolm swung it back down with all his strength. As the buckle connected with my ribs, I heard a loud crack and pain lanced through my side. I screamed.

THE PAIN STARTLED ME AWAKE, and I struggled to breathe. Touching my side, I panicked when my fingers came away with blood. Staring wide-eyed at my fingers, I checked my room. It was empty, everything as it had been, but breathing hurt and I was bleeding where the buckle connected.

Struggling through immense pain, I made my way to the bathroom and lifted my singlet top. Black bruising covered the side of my ribs, and a cut was weeping. Strangling down my scream of anguish, I moved gingerly to my bed to find my phone.

"Vera?" Jeremy's voice came over the line, half asleep.

It was hard to stop crying long enough to talk. "I, I think I need a doctor."

Wide awake now, Jeremy's voice lost the sound of sleep. "What?"

More sobs burbled from my throat. "He found me."

"Are you at the cottage?"

"Yes."

"We'll be there in a moment."

Dropping my phone, I huddled against the side of my bed. My

instinct was to apply pressure to the bleeding, but if I'd broken a rib, I didn't want to risk displacing it.

"Vera?" Dale's voice called from the back door. "Shit, it's locked. Vera?"

Drawing a breath to call back, pain seared through my side, and I cried out in pain instead.

"Vera!" Dale sounded frantic. "Give those to me."

A moment later, Dale was running into my room, his pants on and sans shirt. Bob and Jeremy behind him. "What happened?"

Lifting my singlet, I watched them all gasp in surprised horror. "He knows I survived. I dream real. In my dream, he found me and beat me with his belt."

Forehead drawing down, Bob tilted his head. "Are you sure you didn't fall?"

Dale held up his hand. "Vera, does he know where you are?"

"He'd be here if he did."

Accepting my explanation without hesitation, Dale nodded. "He'll be looking for you now." Dale looked to Jeremy. "Call Jonathan and get him to come over."

Stepping out of the room, Jeremy pulled out his phone and started talking.

Bob frowned. "You believe Malcolm did that?"

"Lycan females have a history of the goddess walking their dreams. Sometimes what she shows them comes back to the waking world with them."

"I always thought I must have dream walked, or he drugged me before hurting me, so I thought I was dreaming. But the first time I woke injured was the week before Malcolm became alpha. I didn't tell anyone because who would believe that insanity?"

Bob paled. "So, Malcolm beats her in her dream, she suffers it for real?"

Dale nodded and came to my side. He lifted my singlet and examined the wound. "You said he used a belt? Do you think he broke your rib?" I whimpered. "Okay, our doctor is on the way, Vera."

Sobbing into my bedspread, I gripped it in my fist. "How did this happen? I was so careful covering my tracks."

Putting his arm around me, Dale was careful not to put pressure on my injury. "I don't know." Holding me, Dale repositioned my face to his chest. Crying into his shoulder, my breath hitched on the spikes of pain from my ribs.

The doctor came an hour later. Jeremy letting him in. "Sorry, I was at work when you called. What happened?" Jeremy filled him in, then the doctor came to sit by me as Dale extracted himself.

"I'm Jonathan, the pack doctor, can I have a look?" When I nodded, he lifted my top to examine me.

Inhaling his scent of earth and musk, I exhaled and cringed. "You're pack too?"

"I am." Feeling around my injury, Jonathan concurred the rib was likely fractured. Turning his head to look at Dale, the doctor raised a brow. "This is your mate, right?" Dale nodded. "And she's full-blooded?"

"Can you not smell her?" Bob asked, exasperated.

Jonathan tapped his nose. "I was dealing with a blue bloater when you called. All I'm going to be smelling for a few days is a dead, drowned guy."

"She's full Lycan," Dale confirmed.

"Well, that's easier. Just bind with her, and she'll heal overnight."

Jaw tense, Dale gritted his teeth. "I won't do it without her permission."

Jonathan seemed lost. "What do you mean? She's your mate, protocol requires you to mark her and bind your life to hers. As a full blood female, you should have done it on the first meeting, since they are all the more precious."

Glancing up to meet Dale's eyes, I noted the rigidness of his posture, almost as if he was the one in pain. This is what he meant by protocols, and by not recognizing him. "It's okay."

"It's not okay, Vera. Once I mark you, bind with you, that will marry us. You aren't ready for that yet."

"Dale, I would agree to a mass orgy with you all right now if it stopped the pain."

"That's exactly what I mean. This is a lifelong bind, Vera. You can't agree to it just to heal a rib. Tomorrow morning, your rib would heal, but our mating would stay. If you had sex with Bob or Jeremy again, our laws entitle me to kill them."

"Wait, what?" Jeremy's eyes popped wide open.

"We didn't have sex," Bob defended, looking very guilty.

"I can smell both of you all over her." Dale pointed to Bob. "I could smell your combined scents of lust by the back door. And you, I can smell all over her and this room." He jabbed a finger at Jeremy.

"I didn't have sex with her!" both men defended. "I haven't even kissed her," Jeremy argued. Bob fell quiet and took a step back. Jeremy looked at Bob with wide eyes. "You kissed her?"

"She kissed me. You've smelled her. It's near impossible to resist her."

Dale's jaw was grinding hard, but I was resisting laughing, mainly because it would hurt even more.

"Take it outside." Directing them with a finger jabbed towards the door, Jonathan glared at them all. The three men complied.

"So, rest and pain killers?" I asked the doctor to focus my mind elsewhere.

"Not your first fractured rib?"

"Not by far." Though, not as often as you'd think. Broken bones meant longer recovery time, and Malcolm wasn't that patient. Malcolm was very good at only causing soft tissue injuries. The others who occasionally got to beat me weren't so refined in their beatings.

"If you aren't willing to let our alpha mark you, then I'll prescribe some pain killers for you..."

"They don't work. I'll make birch leaf tea, it's the most effective for relieving this sort of pain."

Jonathan took out a pad and gauze. "I'll clean this wound up and dress it and get out of your way then."

Grimacing, I lay as still as possible while Jonathan worked. "How come you weren't at dinner on Saturday?"

"I was on duty." Cleaning the wound, Jonathan met my eyes. "Why won't you mate with Dale?"

"Trust issues. Plus, I thought I was human until today." Jonathan frowned. "I only found out we are our own species today. Even when I realized Dale was old, it didn't occur to me, that if I'm the same, I'd also age well."

Jonathan started packing up his gear. "I'm going to give you some life advice. Since I'm your doctor, you should take it. Allow Dale to mark you. Besides the healing ability it will give you, it will protect you. Worry about the mating stuff later."

"Dale and I aren't going to happen. The last thing I need is another alpha male who thinks he can control me."

"But he's your mate? Surely you feel the connection, the draw to each other?"

Thinking of how my body tingled with his touch, and my dreams of Dale, I turned my face away. "Perhaps, I'm broken?"

"Passion finds us all, eventually."

CHAPTER 10

"Would you like me to stay?"

Eyeing where Dale stood by my bed, I concentrated on trying to relax with each breath. "No. Could you ask Jeremy to try and source some birch leaf for me, please? I'll need it for pain."

"I'll make sure you get it tomorrow." There was a pregnant pause. "Why did you kiss Bob? Are you attracted to him?"

"Am I female and have a heartbeat?" Bob was gorgeous. He had nothing on Dale, but still. Any of this pack could be models, and most were.

"I see." Shoving his hands in his pockets, Dale glared at the floor, his anger flaring.

"No, you don't."

"Then make it a little less obscure for me, Vera. Why does Bob appeal to you over me?" His anger ramping up a notch, hesitating, then backing down, like Dale was struggling to control it.

"He's not an alpha."

"You can't paint us all with the same tainted brush, Vera."

"You imprisoned me in my home. You painted yourself."

Dale was quiet. "You are my mate. I've been struggling for months to cope with the fact that you aren't feeling what I'm feeling. The idea of letting you up and leave my life-"

"So, trapping me here was the solution? Taking away my free will, giving me no other option but to do what you wanted. That was the best way to deal with your feelings?" God forbid a man actually considers how I felt.

"It's the solution I had available to me. We prepared the injunction to stop you buying the land. Cameron came to the hospital to give you the last chance to sell the property. If you still refused, he was going to serve you with the injunction. When he saw you and caught your scent, he called me and told me you were one of us."

"So, you allowed me to buy the house so you could draw me into your pack?"

"It was obvious you needed a place to go, Vera. If I didn't take you in, another pack would have stumbled across you and taken you instead." He shifted his stance and avoided my eyes. "I didn't mean to attack you that first night. The wolf was in control when you scared away his dinner. It wasn't until I was standing over you that I caught your scent and realized you were my mate."

Dale moved closer to where I lay on the bed. "When I saw your body covered with those bruises, I was furious. It was the only reason I held back from shifting and marking you then and there."

"Thank you for having enough control to resist that," I whispered, a little terrified of how bad my first night here could have been.

"Thank you for agreeing to stay."

"Jeremy convinced me to stay, not you. Thank him."

Dale stopped moving closer. "Should I ask how Jeremy convinced you?"

Tears threatened to spill with the admission. "He showed me how weak and vulnerable I am. That's not going to change by going some-where else."

With his brow's pinching above his nose, Dale looked confused.

"Goodnight, Dale. Lock my door on the way out please." My eyes fluttered closed, unable to stay awake any longer.

A FEW HOURS LATER, the pain in my ribs woke me. Making my way to the bathroom, I washed my face clean and then made my way out to the kitchen. Feet stopping, I stared at the image before me.

Dale stood looking out the kitchen window wearing only a pair of tracksuit pants. When he lifted the coffee cup to his lips, all the muscles in his back shifted. His olive skin was glowing in the morning light. I almost felt the need to take a photo of him because it was that perfect a pose. Frowning, I glared at his back. He chuckled.

"You knew I was here?"

He finally turned around with a satisfied smirk on his face. "I always know when you are near. Can't you tell when I'm here?"

When I shook my head, Dale's smile dropped, his eyes blinking several times. Going to the fridge, I dug out some aspirin, dissolving four into a glass of water.

"Jeremy's having trouble finding a store that sells the birch leaf."

Glancing at him, I noticed the way he stood. Feet apart, one hand in his pocket, the other holding the coffee mug. He looked just as delicious from the front. Biting my lip, my eyes traced the gullies and rises of his abdomen. Snapping out of my trance, I caught Dale smirking as he lifted the mug to his beautiful luscious lips.

"Oh, my god! You used to model, didn't you?"

Dale seemed amused. "Yes. That's how I got into the business."

Shaking my head, I went to my notepad at the table. "Can you put a shirt on? This isn't a photoshoot."

"You have any men's clothes here, do you?" Dale raised an eyebrow.

"Your house isn't even a kilometer away."

"Now, how would that be fair?" Dale moved closer to me while I wrote on the notepad, his voice dreamy and full of all things naughty. "Why should I wear clothes when you aren't?"

Peering down at myself, I frowned in confusion. "I'm in my pajamas."

"So am I," Dale smirked. "Kind of."

Now, I imagined Dale naked, and on top of me. Thankfully, I tried to take a deep breath, and pain speared me back to my senses. Gasping, I gripped the table. Sobering, Dale went to touch me.

"Don't!" Ripping off the piece of paper, I held it out for him. "This is where I used to order the birch leaf. I need a shower."

WHEN I CAME out of my bedroom next, Dale had showered and dressed in jeans and a t-shirt. I groaned internally. The guy got sexier every time I saw him. "Jeremy has gone to get the birch leaf. Do you need anything else while he's in the city?"

"A new perfume. Something that stinks and will scare dogs away."

"Then you wouldn't be able to wear it. Your natural scent is intoxicating to our kind."

"Hence, the need for something to mask it. Aren't you meant to be at work?"

"You're more important."

"Don't do that."

Dale pulled up a chair opposite where I sat on the lounge. "We need to talk."

This time I groaned out loud.

"If your father raised you right, you would know the protocol for finding your mate. You would have recognized it the first time we met. My scent would calm you, relieve your anxiety, and it would also make you...amorous."

Thinking of the hankie Jeremy gave me, and the way I relaxed in Dale's bedroom. Then there were the thoughts I had of Dale and me in his bedroom.

"At sixteen, your father should have arranged your introduction to the packs. The members would have lined up near the door. As Alpha, I would have greeted you first and sniffed your neck. If I hadn't recognized you as my mate, I would have then introduced the rest of my pack one by one. But, I would have, and you would have offered me your neck. It would have been instinct, even if you were not

74

instructed to do so. I would mark you as mine. We would celebrate that night, and then you would be a member of my pack."

"Would you expect me to sleep with you that first night?" The idea creeped me out a little.

Dale shook his head. "The mating comes when both are ready. It usually doesn't take long due to the effect our scents have on each other. Plus, sixteen-year-old girls can be quite enslaved by their desires." Lips turning down, Dale sat forward in his chair to lean on his knees. "That is the protocol. And it's done like that for a reason.

"As I've already told you, females of our kind are rare, and they always have a mate. They are also more vulnerable and dangerous to their pack. Once a female of our kind matures, her scent is intoxicating. It drives our males mad if she remains unmated. They become aggressive, fighting amongst each other to get mating rights."

"Wait, you're insinuating that how I've Malcolm treated me is my fault?"

"No! Your father caused it by hiding you. Malcolm is at fault because he should have followed protocol."

"He raped me when I was fourteen. He was never going to follow protocol!" Wincing, I regretted taking the breath.

Body rigid, Dale closed his eyes as his rage pulsed and withdrew. Taking a few steady breaths, Dale opened his eyes again. The brown pushed his indigo to the outer edges of his irises, and the gold wolf eyes suffused around the pupil.

"I believe you are right. What I'm trying to explain, is that your pack never used to be a house of brutes. Under your father's rule, they were well ordered. Even after Malcolm became Alpha, they didn't decline for several more years. But, as you matured, your pheromones became a drug in the pack-house. One that induced the men to fight for the right to, for lack of a better word, mount you."

Remembering the yelling and fighting, I struggled to swallow.

Dale's eyes intensified as he watched tears form in my eyes. "You were living in a house of drug addicts, all willing to kill to get their fix."

"But I was with Malcolm? And they didn't have sex with me, they beat me."

Dale's hands clenched in tight fists. "Malcolm never marked you, he couldn't, you weren't his mate. The mark would have festered and made you both sick. So, you were an unmated female. Malcolm's violence probably escalated because he was continuously challenged. I've heard that happened often. By letting the others beat you, it provided them with a mini-dose. Like a heroin addict at the methadone clinic. Your pain and fear would have also dampened your pheromones. Of course, the smell of your fear is like a red flag to a bull, so it amplified a different rage."

Now, I was crying. Reaching out tentatively, Dale encased my hands in his. "Malcolm brought the state of his pack on himself. I can't do it to mine."

When I looked up confused, Dale licked his lips. "You haven't been here anywhere near as long, but my pack is already reacting to your pheromones. Howard responded straight away. He was a drug addict in the seventies and is more susceptible to having his buttons pushed. I didn't expect it to hit him so hard. His aggression towards you is because he wants you, but knows you belong to me.

"Bob is my delta. When you kissed him, it took all his strength to resist you, Vera. Even Jeremy has become very protective of you. As my beta, he is the strongest second to me, and yet he still rubbed his scent all over you."

Sitting back, Dale removed his hands from mine. "I can't let you leave, Vera. I'm your mate. You are also a danger to any other pack that finds you. Your presence would turn them into vicious wild animals like it did your old pack. However, you are affecting my pack even when you aren't in the same house. I need to ask you to allow me to mark you. We can go without mating for now. But, for the sake of my pack, I need to mark you as mine and dampen your pheromones, so they only affect me."

Sitting there crying, I heard everything he was telling me, and it made sense. My pack grew more violent over the years. The way the men leered at me and how they touched me if they got me away from

Malcolm made sense. I didn't need Dale to convince me what he said was true.

The memory of Jeremy storming into my house yesterday, holding me against the wall played in my mind. Did that happen because he smelled Bob on me? "If we do this, will there be side effects?" I didn't want to see Jeremy and Bob turn into the monsters of my nightmares.

"The dreams of us being intimate may increase."

My cheeks grew hot, and so did my chest. "You know about those?"

Dale smirked. "Yes, Vera. I get them too."

My entire body flamed thinking of how hot those dreams were and the image of Dale having them made me squirm in my seat.

Dale cleared his throat; possibly to rid his mind of those dreams. "Our attraction to each other will become more intense, but I won't act on it until you are ready. Your years of trauma have allowed you to subdue your natural response to being near me. So, you will resist me longer than any other female newly mated."

"You won't turn violent?"

"My scent calms you, and being bound to you will make me more balanced. We are yin and yang, Vera. We will balance each other."

"Soul mates?"

"That is the romanticized idea, yes." Dale's eyes were bright indigo again. He took a deep breath. "Will you allow it?"

"It will help my pain, too, right?" I could barely say no and watch Bob and Jeremy turn into mean bastards. If I got a quick healing solution out of it and I wasn't expected to sleep with him or move into the pack-house...wait! Check that.

"You'll heal after a good long sleep."

"I can stay living here in the cottage. I don't have to move into the pack-house?"

"For now, you need your space and your isolation."

He wanted to keep me away from his pack in case my proximity still set them off. "Will it hurt?"

"Momentarily. I'm told the experience is euphoric for the female after the initial penetration."

Waiting as I bit my lip to think it over, Dale sat watching me.

When I finally nodded, Dale stood holding out his hand. "Let's go to your room, so you can be comfortable."

"ou said this would happen on greeting me, correct?" Still holding my hand, Dale nodded. "That would be by the door." Disentangling my hand from his, I moved to the door and turned to face him. "Let's do this how it should have been." Translation: I'm not comfortable lying on my bed with you.

Lips tilting up a little, Dale moved to join me. "Okay." Standing over me, he gave me a reassuring smile. "I'm going to sniff you now."

There was a glint of mischief in his eyes that made me pause. "Hang on. When you sniffed my crutch as Alpha, and then you tried to nuzzle my neck...?"

Dale gave a quiet chuckle. "Guilty."

"I'd smack your face if it wouldn't hurt me so much."

Still chuckling, Dale lowered his face and sniffed my neck. His nose brushed my collarbone, then trailed up my neck behind my ear and into my hair. My breathing hitched. Dale released a soft growl of appreciation.

Dropping my gaze to the floor, I noticed his physical appreciation. Closing my eyes, I allowed Dale to move my face to his neck. "Breathe me in, Vera."

Inhaling, I brushed my nose up his neck as he did to me. Instantly, my body relaxed, and my head became dizzy. Recognizing his scent from the handkerchief and the way it affected me. Tingling broke out across my back and abdomen as Dale wrapped his arm around my left side to support my back. When he moved closer, I hung my head back and to the side as Dale lowered his mouth to my neck.

"Don't hurt me."

"Never." Kissing the vulnerability of my pulse, Dale opened his mouth. A snapping and cracking sound that sounded like his jaw filled my ears. For a moment, I panicked and started to push away. Dale's scent grew stronger, enfolded me in his will, and kept my body docile in his hold.

My eyes startled wide when thick canines bit into my shoulder, right where it joined my neck. There was a sensation of startling pain, but something more powerful washed it away. Closing my eyes, images of Dale and I together played like a trailer for a romance film. Kissing and laughing in his kitchen as I cooked us breakfast, swimming in the pool, in his bed. The image of me heavy with child, Dale's arms holding me as he kissed my belly, morphed into me holding our child in my arms.

"A baby," I whispered with a smile. Opening my eyes, Dale was looking down at me with awe in his eyes. "You're going to give me a child." Closing my eyes again, the visions of our future together stole me into a peaceful sleep.

Waking with a sense of happiness, I blinked a little to see me staring up at the bedroom ceiling. My smile vanished as I cleared my head of the dream and looked around confused. Sitting up in bed, my side pulled a little, but it didn't hurt. It was dark, so I turned on the light. An origami wolf head sat on my bedside table. Frowning, I picked it up and, noticing words written on the paper, I unraveled it.

VERA,

I needed to go. Rest tomorrow to let that rib heal better. Have dinner with me tomorrow night?

Dale.

. . .

Sighing, I took the note with me to the kitchen. I was making myself hot milk when I saw movement behind me reflected in the window. Jumping, I dropped the milk and turned around to see Jeremy standing there. My heart was hammering in my throat as I tried to steady my breathing enough to tell him off.

"You need to be more aware of your surroundings. Though, I'm glad to see you're not in pain anymore."

Nodding, I still wasn't able to talk.

"Dale asked me to stay and make sure you were okay after you woke."

"Am I safe to be around now?"

"More than you were before; still not beyond a weaker man's interest." Jeremy looked at the floor. "Can I help you clean that up?"

Glancing down at the milk carton spilling on the floor, I blinked at it a few times. Squatting, I picked it up to stop the entire thing emptying. Jeremy was beside me with paper towel wiping it up. "My heads still a little fuzzy."

"I remember how high you were on the handkerchief; the real thing would be longer-lasting." Sighing as if something had been bothering him, Jeremy paused to watch me. "Don't feel guilty for what happened with your pack. That was never your fault."

I kept my eyes downcast.

Standing up, Jeremy disposed of the milk drenched toweling. "Starting Saturday, I'm going to begin training you in self-defense. Four days a week, I work with Dale in the city, so I can only train you on the weekend and Wednesday's. You'll need to practice what I teach you with Bob on the other days."

Unsure about training with Bob now, I stood up and turned my back.

"He's a delta, Vera. They are third in line and strong enough to be beta if they focus themselves. Bob will be strong enough to resist you. Just don't go tempting him to annoy Dale anymore, okay?"

Taking the milk carton out of my hand, Jeremy took over making my hot milk for me. Not arguing, I curled up on the lounge and watched outside.

"Here." Jeremy handed me the milk and sat down. "Do you feel his absence?" Thinking about it and shook my head. "What do you feel?"

"Woozy, and like I'm hollowed out." Placing my hand over my stomach, I checked to make sure my insides were solid. "Scooped empty to my core."

Jeremy exhaled in relief. "Do yourself a favor. For the next week, write down the times that feeling comes and goes, or any other feeling you have."

"Are you worried?"

"More running an experiment to see if anything changes for you now." Picking up the television remote, Jeremy started flicking through channels. "You should keep a diary, compare how you used to react to things, to how you do now."

Wondering why, I blinked a few times but decided he might have a good point. "Okay, I'll give it a go."

"Do you own a diary?"

"With the potential of Malcolm finding it? Hell, no!"

Leaning over the arm of the lounge, Jeremy retrieved a shopping bag. "I thought that would be the case." Pulling out a small container, he placed it on the coffee table. "Birch leaf, in case you need it again." Then he handed me a beautiful journal with an expensive-looking pen. "I was in the city when Dale told me you agreed. I thought this would come in handy for you."

"Thank you." I blinked back the tears. "I... I mean, no one has ever given me something unless it was to benefit them."

"This is to benefit Dale and yourself. It will allow you to see how the bond between you works. I'm practical, not sentimental."

When I smirked, Jeremy raised a brow. "I was thinking, I kissed the wrong pack member."

Jeremy snorted. "No, you picked the perfect one. If you had picked me, Dale would have known it was a ploy. By picking Bob, you devalued Dale, and made me get all possessive, which also worked in your favor."

"Did he really think I wouldn't fight back?"

"You've spent your life beaten down. Of course, he did." Jeremy didn't even try to sugar coat it. "But that's not why he did it, Vera."

"He told me why." It was a lot to take on. "It's why I agreed to this." My hand covered where Dale had bitten me. There wasn't any marks or scabs, only tenderness of bruising under the flesh.

Nodding, Jeremy stopped flicking channels. "Why is everything chick flicks tonight?"

Smiling, I snuggled into his side. "I like this movie."

"Of course, you do." Watching me yawn, Jeremy placed an arm around my shoulders and cuddled me to his side.

"The books are better."

"They always are." Picking up his mobile with his free hand, Jeremy typed out a message. "I can get you some books tomorrow if you like?"

"I can buy my own."

Watching the movie, I already felt my tears building.

"You're not going to cry, are you?"

"From the moment he dies until she meets the new guy. It happens every time I watch it."

"Next time we do a movie night, I'm bringing DVDs." When his phone pinged, Jeremy read the message then relaxed back on the lounge and watched the movie with me.

OPENING MY EYES, I jolted away from the arm around me. Jeremy jumped as if bitten and looked down at me, half asleep. "What is it?"

"Nothing, I just..." *was letting you touch me,* "hadn't realized I'd fallen asleep." Moving away from Jeremy, I went to the kitchen, pouring us both a drink of water.

Scrubbing his face, Jeremy turned off the television and stifled a yawn. "It's a little before dawn, so I'll head home and get a few hours' of sleep in my own bed."

"Can I ask a question?"

"Sure."

"Why can't I turn into a wolf?"

Jeremy shrugged. "No one knows."

"Can Hymn and Alexia?"

"They do a partial shift." Picking up the glass of water I'd poured for him, Jeremy took a big long drink. I stood there, waiting for further explanation. Jeremy finished the glass and frowned at me before his brows lifted. "Oh, right. They can grow the teeth and claws, and their eyes change to have night vision. No one knows why, but we've always thought it was because they are only half-breeds."

"So, why can't I?"

Jeremy blinked at me. "Who says you can't? Yes, you haven't done it so far, but you smell like us, so there is no reason you can't change like us."

My brows furrowed. "Has any full-blooded females ever changed before?"

Shaking his head, Jeremy turned, walking out. "No, but there's always a first for everything. Why not give it a try? Goodnight."

The door closed behind him, leaving me staring after him wondering what the hell that meant. Deciding Jeremy was still half asleep, I locked the back door and went back to bed. Unable to sleep, I grabbed my laptop and started researching Lycans.

CHAPTER 12

The knock at the front door surprised me. With a frown, I went to the front door and cracked it open a little. When Dale stood there dressed in his suit, I opened it wider.

"You're earlier than I expected. I haven't even put dinner in the oven yet, but I guess we can talk while I cook."

"Cook?" Dale stayed by the door, his face conveying his confusion. "Didn't you get my letter about dinner tonight?"

"Of course, I was just saying I hadn't put it in the oven yet." Turning, I walked back to the kitchen to keep preparing dinner.

"Um, Vera. I wasn't expecting you to cook for me."

"Then how is it dinner if we don't eat?"

Catching up at the end of the hall, Dale rubbed his lips together before taking my hand and looking me in the eye. "I've booked a table at a nice restaurant for us."

Staring at Dale, I blinked in confusion.

After a moment Dale took a breath and cursed. "Vera, have you never gone out for dinner on a date?"

The question felt like a slap. "No, I haven't."

Sighing, Dale searched my eyes. "I love your cooking, but would the food keep until tomorrow night?"

Blinking repeatedly as I realized Dale was going to take me out and that I wouldn't have to cook, or clean, or... "Yes, I can put it in the fridge." As I wrapped everything up and placed it in the fridge, a butterfly fluttered around my insides.

Once I'd cleaned up, I took off my apron and looked down at myself. "Should I change?"

Considering his answer, Dale looked me over. "You look beautiful, but you may feel more comfortable in the dress you wore last Saturday night."

Accepting the assessment, I went to change. Dale ran a modeling agency. He knew what made women look good, so I trusted his judgment. Once I'd changed, I walked out to find him staring out the back window. "Would you prefer my hair up or down?"

Dale turned with a frown. "Vera, wear your hair however it makes you feel comfortable." Moving closer, Dale touched my mouth. I trembled a little with the caress of his thumb across my bottom lip. Easing both his hands to either side of my face, Dale lifted my hair away from it.

"When your hair is up, it highlights your high cheekbones. Which, in turn, draws the eye to your plump lips." Releasing my hair, Dale stood back. "When it's down, you're all eyes." He frowned. "Could I ask you to remove the contacts?"

"No, I'm sorry. Here at home, I'll leave them out for you, but not outside of the house."

Dale nodded in acceptance. "Very well. Are you ready?"

Flipping my head forward, I pulled my hair into a high messy ponytail. "How's this?"

"I could hire you, you look that good. So effortlessly beautiful."

Eyes fluttering, I felt my cheeks heat a little. Taking my hand, Dale led me out to his car; a dark blue Jaguar. Always the gentleman, Dale opened the door for me. When we arrived at the hideaway restaurant thirty minutes later, he opened the door for me again. Dale was right, I would have felt underdressed in my mid-season dress.

We ordered and ate with barely a word edgewise. When we did talk, it was about the places Dale traveled around the world, which seemed to be everywhere. We also discussed my favorite meals to cook, both for taste or ease of making the dish.

We drove home again in the same silence. Dale seemed perturbed by something and kept frowning during the drive. At my place, he walked me back to the front door. "Did you want to come in for a coffee?"

Dale's lips twitched. "Ah, um, coffee will keep me awake all night."

"I make a mean hot chocolate with brandy."

"How can I say no to that?"

Smiling, I unlocked my door. Following me in, Dale locked the door behind him. Kicking my shoes off in my bedroom, I went to the kitchen. Mixing sugar, cocoa, potato starch, and milk, I then heated it. Once I felt the mixture start to thicken, I turned off the heat and set out the hot chocolate mugs. Adding in a splash of brandy, I stirred it through. Pouring the thick liquid chocolate into the cups, I placed in vanilla straw wafers and served it up.

"It's too hot for a while, so let it cool down," I warned before turning my back to clean up, humming to myself as I did.

"I like that song. What's it called?" Freezing, I realized what song I'd been humming. "Begin Again, right? About getting over a bad relationship by meeting a nice guy."

"You know that song?" I asked, deflecting the meaning behind his words.

"I have two daughters and work in a building with a lot of young females. I get exposed to all sorts of things most men my age would not."

"Most men, your age are dead."

"Touché." Chuckling, Dale picked up the hot chocolate, sipped and moaned. "I haven't had cioccolata calda in over a decade. Did you learn to make it in Italy?"

Blowing over my drink to cool it, I avoided eye contact. "I never left the pack-house. Once a year he'd take me to a resort or hotel for a few days to celebrate our anniversary. Which was the day he raped me, in case you're wondering? He considered that the start of our relationship. For the first hour out and into the pack-house, Malcolm kept me blindfolded. He always took precautions to ensure I couldn't find my way out should I choose to be stupid enough to try it."

Dale fell quiet.

Grimacing in the sudden thinness of the air, I sighed. "I apologize. I didn't mean to bring that up. I've never left the country."

Lifting his drink to his lips, Dale drank the rest, both of us quiet. When he finished, I watched him lick his lips and felt my knees weaken with the sudden hit of brandy take effect. That's what I was telling myself it was. A howl from far away caught our attention outside. Dale looked towards the manor house. "The pack are letting me know they are heading out to hunt."

When I bit my lip, Dale rose from the kitchen bench and walked around, rinsing his cup clean. "I've told them to keep it away from here." When Dale turned to face me, I gave a slight nod. Dale looked out the window. "I told them I'd join them when I got back."

"Okay." Draining my mug, I put it aside, ready to walk him out. "Thank you for dinner."

With a careful look in his eyes, Dale rubbed the corner of my mouth with his thumb, then he lifted it to his. Watching him suck the chocolate that had been on the edge of my lip, I gripped the bench behind me to keep my body in place. How could he be so damn sexy sucking his thumb?

"It was my pleasure." All the humor was gone from his face. Lust and intensity staring back at me now. Sidling closer, Dale lowered his mouth to mine. That hot chocolate had nothing on the taste of Dale's mouth. It was like I'd drunk several mouthfuls of brandy straight from the bottle. His scent and taste were heady and intoxicating.

Within seconds, the kissing went from *'polite farewell,'* to *'should be taking our clothes off.'* Moments later, I was unbuttoning and pushing Dale's shirt from his shoulders. Moaning, my hands tingled over his muscular chest. Stepping us back until my bum was against the kitchen bench, Dale pressed himself against me. Feeling my body, Dale found the fastener on my dress.

My body temperature soared when Dale slipped his free hand in to touch my bare back as he lowered the zip. Gasping at the sensations his touch was causing, I hung my head back. Dropping his mouth to my neck, Dale kissed over his mark.

Having read up on chemistry, I understood how lust worked. How chemical changes in the body incited stimulation in our muscles and cells. But until now, I'd never experienced lust-induced galvanism myself. My nerves fired, and my body pulsed with desire.

Moaning Dale's name as he pushed my dress to the floor, I stood there panting in my underwear. Dale's eyes wandered my body. "You are the most beautiful thing I've ever laid my eyes on, Vera." Capturing my face in his hands, Dale kissed me slow and deep.

If I thought I'd come undone before, I was the moment he kissed me like that. He explored my mouth with tenderness, kissing me with the patience of a saint and the intentions of a devil. I was a woman possessed. Pure, primal, lust scorched through my body. Pressing against him, I yearned for this magnificent man to plunder me.

Making light work of Dale's belt and fly, I shoved his pants to the floor. Lifting me to the kitchen bench, Dale moved between my welcoming thighs. We were both breathing heavy. Holding my face in his hands, Dale gazed down on me; his eyes the brightest I'd ever seen them.

A howl directly outside startled us both. Taking several steps back, Dale afforded me a view of how magnificent his entire body was. My head cleared, the passion of the moment broken by the interference. Dropping from the bench, I grabbed up my dress holding it up in front of me.

"Goddess, Vera, I'm so sorry. I didn't intend for anything to happen tonight."

The howl came from outside again, this time immediately followed by another.

The lust fading, I shuddered at having the wolves this close to my house again. "Your pack are waiting for you."

Mouth tightening, Dale glared towards the window. "Pack of cock-blockers is what they are." Snatching up his clothes, Dale stepped into me and kissed me. Only for a minute, but my entire body felt light as a feather by the time his lips withdrew. "I also need to get you some blinds. Jeremy says the underwear is much nicer on you than the mannequin."

Eyes bulging at the comment, I tried to cover myself better. My entire body flamed, exposing my embarrassment.

With a smirk, Dale gave me a quick peck on the lips. "I'll see you for dinner tomorrow night." Pure heat and intent in his eyes.

Staring at my kitchen sink, I tried to calm my racing heart and heaving lungs. The quaking in my body I'd given up on stopping. I figured, once Dale was gone, that would die down.

"I'm going to leave my clothes on your back porch if you don't mind?"

Turning, I watched Dale unlock the back door. "That's fine."

Grinning at me, Dale stepped outside. Dropping his clothes, Dale jogged down the steps into the yard. When he disappeared out of sight, I moved forward with a frown to see what happened. A gasp escaped when the big black dog I'd known as alpha stood in Dale's place. Yes, I knew they were one and the same, but the change was quick. Nothing like I'd imagined. Watching alpha run off into the woods, I felt a little of the happiness of the night fade away. Picking up the journal Jeremy gave me, I noted the change in emotion. Then, taking the diary to my room, I wrote how being with Dale made me feel.

At first, I didn't assess it, just wrote everything down and then went to change for bed. When I'd locked up the house and crawled into bed, I read what I'd written. Closing the journal stunned, I sunk down in bed, terrified and awed simultaneously. Mixed reactions and feelings encased me in a cloud of confusion and doubt. Did I trust what I'd written, or become more cautious?

As I closed my eyes, my body overrode my brain, and I drifted off, remembering the way Dale kissed and touched me.

'Trust him.' My heart urged.

'What's trust?'

CHAPTER 13

Standing in the kitchen making myself breakfast, I realized I was smiling at nothing. Having slept well, I'd woken happy, but now I was feeling even better. Eyes drawn to the backyard, I noticed Dale emerging from the forest path. Dressed in a pair of knee-length shorts and a polo shirt, with volleys on his feet, Dale looked good. Remembering how much better he'd looked naked brought a fresh hit of heat to my cheeks.

Jogging up the back steps, Dale knocked on the back door. Placing my coffee on the bench, I walked to the door, opening the glass door, but leaving the screen locked. "We agreed on dinner, not breakfast."

"I ate a while ago. I was hoping we could spend the day together?"

"Doing what, exactly?"

Dale's smile grew. "I was thinking of taking the yacht out."

Unsure if he was having a go, I blinked at him. Then the buzzer on my oven sounded startling me. "Come in."

Unlocking the door, I rushed to the oven and removed my poached eggs. Serving them onto my plate, I added the toast and took it to the table. Considering Dale, I scanned my meal, wondering if I should make him something.

"Sit and eat, I'll steal some of your coffee."

Sitting, I started eating, and Dale joined me at the table with his coffee,

"So, as I was saying, I have a yacht. With this being such a nice day, I thought you may want to join me."

"I've never been on a boat before."

"I figured. I'm going to date you, Vera. I want to show you the world outside a pack-house, show you how to live and enjoy life."

Twirling my knife on my plate, I drew circles in the yolk. I couldn't help my skepticism. "Before you lock me back up in another pack-house? So this time I know what I'm missing out on?"

Dale's anger trickled into the room like a soft hot breeze. "I would never do that to you. When we marry, you will be my wife. You will be free to shop when you like, go to university and study, and you will travel with me around the world. It is no less than my first wife did, Vera. I have the photos to prove it if you wish?"

Trying to discern any lie or trick to his words, I studied him, but I found nothing. Dale seemed genuine. Focusing back on my breakfast, I avoided Dale's eyes. "I can't swim."

"You will have a life vest. I promise you will be safe." I kept staring at the yolk I'd mutilated. Waiting for several breaths, Dale touched my hand with tenderness. "Will you come sailing with me, Vera?"

Meeting his caring eyes, I bit my lip. Happiness was bubbling inside me, but it was such a strange feeling.

"I've asked Jeremy and Bob to come as well if that makes you feel better?"

A small smile tilted my lips as I nodded. "Okay, but if I fall in and drown, I'll haunt you for the rest of your long life."

Dale laughed. "I still win either way."

Not sure I had anything for the occasion, and unsure what people even wore on yachts, I assessed his clothes. "What should I wear?"

"Something summery. You'll need sunscreen and a hat since I doubt your skin has ever seen sunlight. We'll stop at a shop on the way if you need."

Joy almost bursting from my chest, I pressed my hands between my thighs to restrain myself. "Okay. When do we leave?"

"As soon as you are ready." Dale was grinning. "Bob and Jeremy are already there getting the yacht ready."

"So, if I had said no...?"

Dale's eyes sparkled. "Why would you say no to living, Vera?"

Unable to restrain the smirk on my face, I picked up my fork again. It was a very correct statement. I'd spent my current life, not living. It was time I knew what I'd missed.

Finishing my breakfast, I then went into my room and dressed. I chose a turquoise summer dress with a white cardigan to fight off the chill of the morning. When I came out, Dale was smiling at me like I was his birthday cake. My cheeks and chest grew a little warm. Moving closer, Dale took me in entirely, but when his eyes met mine, his smile dimmed at the presence of my contacts.

"Do you have swimmers?"

"Sort of pointless when you can't swim. Plus," my hand went to my right side, "I'm kind of disfigured."

Brows drawing down, his eyes bled to brown, pushing that indigo out to the outer edge of his iris. The thinning oxygen in the room warned of his anger, leaving me trembling in his grasp.

"You are not disfigured. Scars are our past. They show that we have one. Never feel ashamed of that scar, Vera. It's the mark of a free woman."

Eyes filling with tears, I no longer feared his anger but felt blown away by his passion. With tenderness, Dale caressed my face, his thumb brushing under my watery eyes. With a sigh, his anger dissipated. "How are the ribs? Forgive me for not asking yesterday. I was nervous about our date."

Liking the idea of him being nervous about anything, I smirked. Dale always seemed so confident and in control. "Um, good. They don't hurt at all anymore, and the bruising is only minor now." Brushing my hand over the ribs, my happiness seeped away as I remembered Malcolm and his belt buckle. The memory slivered down my spine and made me shiver. "What happens if he finds me?"

Guiding me into a hug, Dale held me with his mouth at my ear. "He won't, so don't worry about it. If he does, it doesn't matter. He can't take you, we are mates, and I will protect you. I will ensure no harm ever comes to you again, Vera."

Breathing in Dale's scent, my body relaxed in his arms. Tensing, Dale chuckled. "Vera, if you want to go sailing, you need to stop doing that. Right now, my instinct is to take you into your bedroom and mate with you. I'm fighting this as hard as I can, but I can't do that if you rub yourself on me like that."

Realizing more than my face had pressed against Dale, I stepped out of his grasp, face hot. "Sorry."

Dale was trying to resist laughing as he watched me blush. His uplifted lips pressed together, and his indigo eyes glittered. "Come on. Let's get going."

We walked out to Dale's car, still parked in front of my place from last night. Driving us east to the sea, Dale stopped at a shop when we hit the beachside town not far from the harbor. Grabbing fifty-plus sunscreen, I then browsed a selection of hats. While I made my choice, Dale disappeared to the clothing section. Selecting a broad-brimmed hat, I went to find Dale.

When I found him, Dale held a stunning olive green one-piece swimsuit. It was lace through the abdomen, so it hid my scar and bruising, while still looking feminine.

When I went to pay, Dale leveled me with a look of warning, before he handed over his credit card to the sales assistant. She was a pretty brunette with a gorgeous tan and warm chocolate eyes. There was a slightly exotic look to her, but I couldn't pick it.

"Persian." The girl smiled, flashing perfect white teeth when I asked. "My grandmother was Persian."

Assessing the girl like she was an artwork, Dale looked impressed but walked away for a moment. The girl blushed for him, but Dale didn't notice.

"Your boyfriend is gorgeous." She placed our purchases in a bag while Dale was searching through a rack of women's slip-on beach shoes. "Is it weird dating an older man?"

A bit surprised for a moment, I gawped at her. Dale only looked to be in his mid-thirties, like most of the wolves in his house except his daughters.

"I mean, how did you score such a hot sugar daddy? Did you meet him at university? Oh my god, is he your professor?"

"Um, no. He's my next-door neighbor. How young do you think I am?"

The girl looked intrigued as she tilted her head, assessing me. "Your healthy skin says late teens, maybe early twenties. Your face shape brings you a little closer to twenty. Your body is slim from diet more than exercise, but your legs show good muscle tone in the calves. I'd say you ran track at school and that's about all you do for exercise. So again, I'm leaning towards twenty.

"Nice assessment." Dale reappeared at my side, placing a pair of rubber-soled sandals down. "These two please?"

The girl smiled. "Thanks. I'm studying fitness and health at college. I'm still deciding if I want to be a personal trainer or a beautician."

"Ever considered modeling?"

"Sure, I even sent in a few headshots when I was at school, but no one seemed interested."

Taking a business card out of his wallet after she gave him back his credit card, he handed her the card. "Ask for Danielle and tell her Mr. Hearn asked you to come in."

She looked at the card, amazed. "This isn't a ploy, is it?"

"It's not a job yet either. Danielle will arrange a trial session for you. If the shots come out good and you can walk a catwalk, then the management team will be in contact." Dale collected our bags. "Good luck."

With a smile, Dale took my hand and walked us out of the store. "How often do you do that?"

"Rarely. Only when I see something unique in a person. I have other staff who scout. She's a bit immature for a twenty-year-old, but I've had worse on the books."

"How do you know she's twenty?"

"The same way she guessed your age. Except, unlike you, she

doesn't have genes that slow the aging process. Thus, my assessment will be correct."

Slipping into the car as Dale held the door, I blinked in amazement. "I always thought I looked my age."

"You always thought you were human too." Starting the engine, Dale kept his gaze on his mirrors as if to hide the scowl on his face.

Maneuvering us through the beach and harbor traffic, Dale parked at the yacht club. Retaking my hand, Dale led me to the slip where his yacht was. It wasn't the biggest yacht, but it would definitely come under the category of luxury.

"Morning, Vera." Bob waved from the upper level of the motorized yacht. "Did you have a nice night?"

The smile on his face told me he'd been a witness to Dale and I getting to know each other in the kitchen. Heat creeping into my cheeks which had nothing to do with the sun, I nodded. "It was very revealing."

"For us all," Jeremy countered, with no hint of humor as he offered me his arm to climb aboard on the main deck.

"I'm guessing you were the howler?"

"The second one, yes." Appraising my dress, Jeremy bowed his head. "You look lovely."

Dale led me a few meters away to the deck lounge. "I'll meet you in the flybridge, Jeremy."

With a mocking salute, Jeremy headed for the stairs up to the upper level where Bob had disappeared. Already sitting on the deck lounge were Juliet and Heidi from the first dinner. As we approached, Dale put his mouth to my ear. "They are currently seeing Bob and Jeremy. They thought you might like the female company. I'll be back in a few minutes."

After greeting the two models, Dale left me there to go check on a few things. Feeling shy, I sat and let the women continue their conversation. I'd been around the human women Malcolm's pack brought home to enjoy, but they never talked to me.

"So are you and Dale seeing each other now?" Heidi asked with a glint in her eye.

"Yes."

"He's gorgeous and rich, a real catch."

Juliet rolled her eyes. "He's also very nice, which matters more to Vera than his money or looks. Am I right?"

"I've learned that looks don't always go beyond the flesh. I'd never go out with a man because he was rich or good looking."

Scrunching her nose as if that disgusted her, Heidi looked me over.

Leaning closer to me, Juliet gave me a sly wink. "Not that it hurts if a nice man is also handsome and wealthy."

"Especially if they are hung like a horse." Heidi nudged Juliet, who went bright red. So much for Bob and his claim that he's neutered.

Picking up the water next to her, Juliet frowned. "You know, Dale has never dated any of the women from work."

"I don't work for him."

Both the women frowned at me in confusion. "So, how did you meet him?"

Finding it odd that they'd forgotten how Dale introduced me, I tilted my head. "I'm his next-door neighbor."

"Yes, but, I mean, we thought that was..." Heidi trailed off. "You really don't work for him, you just live next door?"

"Yes." Confused why they found it hard to believe, I decided to clarify further. "Dale's dog attacked me, that's how we met. Actually, I met Bob first. Then Jeremy barged in and started taking care of me." Juliet sniggered, acknowledging that sounded like Jeremy. "And then Dale introduced himself."

"Was it love at first sight?" Heidi asked with enough lilt that I knew was sarcasm.

Laughing at how rocky a start Dale and I had, I grinned. "God, no. We got off to the wrong foot from the word go. He tried to stop me from moving into my house. When I did move in, his dog attacked me, then he started legal action over our shared driveway access. He was an asshole."

"Now that sounds like Dale." Juliet relaxed, and so did Heidi nodding. "I've been dating Bob on and off for years. Dale is one of the few remaining gentlemen in the world, but he is a very successful businessman for a reason."

"He still won you over, though?"

My brows pinched, confused by Heidi's attitude. "Not yet. We only went on our first date last night. We are getting to know each other, that's what today is about."

Huffing into her water bottle, Heidi turned side on to assess the mouth of the harbor as we passed through. Jerking away when a hand touched my shoulder, I jumped around to face my assailant.

Hands held up to show he meant no harm, Dale stood wary. "Easy, Vera. You've been in the sun too long. Come inside, and I'll show you where you can put some sunscreen on and get your hat."

Biting my lip as I stood, I turned away from Juliet's sympathetic gaze. Frowning, Heidi looked confused about the way I reacted to Dale's touch. At a guess; Juliet knew about domestic violence second hand; either her parents or a friend. Heidi; she'd never been physically injured by another soul.

Following Dale inside, we went downstairs where the cabin rooms were.

CHAPTER 14

The room dale led me into was a luxurious cabin room, complete with a large bed and an open plan bathroom. "Wow! I never knew boats could be like this. I should've bought a yacht instead of the house."

Dale smirked. "I doubt you could afford one of these."

"At least I wouldn't have had to worry about neighbors, or pack-houses, or driving people crazy."

Forehead scrunching, Dale stepped forward. "No. But there are lone wolves who would jump at the chance of finding a female of their species alone and unmated."

My mouth fell open as he took the wind from my sails. "So, no matter where I went, or what I did, I was going to end up in the same situation?"

Closing the distance, Dale brushed his nose past and around mine. "No, because I am your mate, Vera. I will never harm you, I will love, spoil, and adore you. No one else is going to make you feel as alive and happy as I will."

My breathing a little heavy, I stared into his eyes. "That's egotistical, to think you are the only man who could make me happy."

Unperturbed, Dale chuckled. "It's the truth." Stepping back, Dale opened the bag to pull out the swimmers. "Go put these on, I'll help you with your sunscreen when you're ready."

Taking the swimmers, I looked around for a screen or anything to change behind.

"I'll keep my back turned."

Checking over my shoulder, Dale was facing the bed removing the tag from the hat and shoes. Licking my lips, I changed as quickly as possible. Once covered, I moved back up to the bed where Dale was waiting, sunscreen in hand. "I'll do your back for you."

Lifting my hair out of the way, I bit my lip when he started rubbing the cream into the exposed skin. His hands felt nice when he started doing my arms and shoulders. Taking a breath, I stepped away from his reach. "I can do the rest, thank you." Not turning to look at him, I breathed deep.

Dale's breathing sounded as labored as mine. "I'll wait upstairs."

Waiting until the door closed, I finished applying the sunscreen. With my dress on, I grabbed up the hat and changed my ballet flats for the sandals, then headed back out and to the main deck.

As I came up the stairs, Dale was leaning in the doorway. His hands were in his pockets, and a small smile on his face as he listened to the others. He seemed at ease.

Moving up next to Dale, I could see Jeremy and Bob sitting with Juliet and Heidi on the outside lounge flirting. Holding my hat clenched in my hands, I studied the interactions to learn what was normal.

Turning that hint of a smile my way, Dale offered me his hand. "I want to show you something."

Taking his hand, Dale led me around to the front of the boat. When we reached the sundeck complete with hot tub, Dale turned to me. Pulling his shirt over his head, he left it on the cushioned expanse of the sunbeds. "You might want to take your dress off if you want it to stay dry." Then he moved to the very front of the boat.

Folding my dress next to his shirt and the hat - since I was sure the hat would blow away at the bow - and followed Dale. "You aren't going to make me do the titanic Kate, and Leo thing are you?"

"I'm not going to make you do anything." He then encouraged me forward with a light chuckle. Placing me in the bow, Dale stepped in behind me, placing his hands at my waist, precisely like in titanic. "It is an experience worth trying, though."

Laughing, I lifted my arms out to the side, closing my eyes.

"Do you trust me?" Dale whispered.

Before I could respond, he picked me up and tossed me overboard. My heart broke at the moment it took me to leave his arms and fall. Screaming, I looked up to see Dale observing me, his eyes smiling, but they dimmed when they saw mine.

Then I hit netting below me, and I rolled breaking the connection. It was a soft landing; the mesh stretching to take my weight and preventing my fall to the sea below. Staring at the water meters below, I lay there amazed that the churning sea hadn't devoured me. When I realized I was lying in a hammock of some kind, I started laughing – more stress relief than joy at this point.

When Dale climbed down beside me, I pulled back to smack his face, but Dale caught my hand. "I'm sorry I scared you. I've learned that if you ask women to jump into the widows net, they won't."

"So, you threw me and let me think you were tossing me overboard?"

Caressing my cheek, Dale's face softened. "I wanted you to experience this, Vera. Sometimes, it's better to beg forgiveness than ask permission." I glared at him. Gazing past my face to the roiling sea, a smile spreading over his face. "Here comes the fun."

Before I a chance to look, a wave roared beneath us as we headed out between the heads. Breaking on the prow of the ship, it splashed us in the netting above. Gasping at the cold water, I turned to watch the next wave coming towards us. We were flying out through the heads of the harbor, soaring above the tempestuous seas.

The waves were guardians of the sea, pushing back against the boat as if to hinder our escape. The yacht, too strong for the protectors, barged its way through their defenses. Despite how I got here, I felt myself smiling as we glided out to sea. The splash of the waves no longer cold, but amplifying my excitement. Cheering with each dousing, I yelled my enjoyment to the angry waves.

Fingers threaded into my hair, startling me when Dale turned my face to his. His eyes were ablaze with happiness and desire. Taking that all in within a blink, I exhaled sharply as his mouth crushed against mine. Melting into his kiss, lust surged through my system. Rolling me, Dale pressed his body against mine, his lips pinching, demanding my mouth open to his.

Moaning, I relinquished, opening my lips only enough for the tip of his tongue to tease my opening. My hands clung to his back, feeling the muscles ripple beneath his skin.

A massive wave crashed against the prow, soaking us in the spray. Soon, the sea calmed beneath us, accepting defeat, and permitting our voyage. Our kissing slowed to match the calmer waves. My heartbeat, moments ago galloping in my chest, tempered to a trot.

Placing a restraining hand to his chest, I pushed, and Dale withdrew. Indigo eyes full of imprisoned passion, warned me of the heat Dale would unleash if I gave him permission.

"That was the most intense sail through the heads I've ever encountered," Dale murmured.

Licking my lips, I struggled to find my voice. "I agree."

Blessing me with a sinful smirk, Dale glanced at my mouth, as if considering another taste, but he resisted. Eyes bright, he caressed my face. "So, forgive me?"

Slamming my palm against his chest in a playful manner, I smirked. "Not yet, but I'll consider your application."

The sound of Dale's laughter made my stomach somersault. "Let's get you back on deck and warmed up."

Using the netting to pull himself up, Dale climbed up to where it connected with the railing. I tried to copy his grace, but anyone who has ever climbed a net before knows, that shit isn't easy.

Waiting patiently by the top of the netting, Dale held the railing.

Stumbling over my own feet and hands, I climbed between him and the boat. As I came beside him, Dale reached for my upper arm and helped me up, ensuring I had a good hold on the railing before he let me go. Scurrying over, I sighed with the relief of being back on deck.

"I understand why women balk at going down there. I wouldn't have been able to climb down there." My legs and arms trembling with a little fear after I'd seen the fall to the water if I missed the netting.

"Hence, why I threw you with no warning." He grazed his fingers over the goosebumps on my arm. "Will you ever regret the experience?"

"Only if you hurt me. Then it will serve as the disastrous moment where having hope became my mistake."

Dale caressed my shoulder like he couldn't resist touching me. "I will never destroy your hope." Taking my hand, he led me to the hot tub. While I climbed into the warm water, Dale retrieved my hat and plonked it on my head. From his shirt, Dale recovered his sunglasses then stepped into the tub with me.

Floating next to him, my eyes watched the scenery as we sailed the coast. The others joined us shortly after. They chatted and laughed about photoshoots the girls had done on boats or involving hot tubs.

Heidi was a swimwear model and had done a lot of shoots on yachts or at the beach. With her lighter skin tone and voluptuous assets, Juliet was an underwear model.

"My first modeling job was as a plus-size model because my hips and bust were above the industry standard. It didn't matter that I was a size eight everywhere but around my breasts. At the time, my curves were not the norm for the modeling world, and they considered fat."

Gaping at Juliet, I couldn't fathom her being plus size anything. "That's ridiculous."

"I know. I almost refused the job, but I'm glad I didn't. I used the shots from that job to apply to other agencies. Most of the others also tagged me as fat and weren't interested. But Mr. Hearn offered me a contract as a lingerie model for an upmarket lingerie store. After twelve months as their second model, I scored the primary contract for the last three years."

An hour later, we headed inside to dry off and dress for lunch. Dale carried my dress to his cabin, my hand in his other. When he led me to the bathroom and started the shower, I stood there watching. Keeping his eyes locked with mine, Dale removed his shorts.

Not daring to drop my gaze, I kept my focus on his eyes. But my cheeks heated with the idea of looking. Stepping toward me, Dale rubbed his hands over my shoulders as he pushed the straps of my swimwear down my arms. His eyes stayed locked with mine, even when my swimsuit was around my waist. His hand slid across my scar as it lowered. Despite how hot I felt at this moment, I shivered.

Dale's eyes didn't move from mine. The brown pushed out a little from the pupil, but that was the only change. His hands moved on, pushing the swimmers down to my thighs. Skimming his touch back to my waist as I stepped out of my swimwear.

Shifting us under the warm water, Dale stood there running his hands through my hair. His fingers massaging and rinsing us clean of the salt sea.

"Have you ever been to the hairdresser?"

"Yes. When I got out of the hospital, and once since I moved here."

"How did you cut your hair before that?"

"They had a mobile hairdresser who came into the house."

With my body pressed to the sultry nakedness of Dale Hearn, I couldn't summon the dejection of my past.

"What is your natural hair color?"

"Strawberry blonde. I used to keep it shorter; no longer than my shoulders. It grew the months I was in the hospital, and I started to like it long."

Dale's lips twitched, his eyes glittering. "I like your hair long. I also like it auburn, it suits your determination."

Avoiding his eyes, I sucked in a breath. Big mistake looking down. Dale's glorious nakedness was standing thick and hard. Water cascaded down Dale's olive skin. The flow along the contours of

Dale's body, highlighting his muscular definition. "God, you're gorgeous!"

"Vera, you're supposed to say that to my face, not staring at my erection." The appendage in question twitched. It's single eye staring straight up at me from where it rested near his belly button. "Vera?" With tenderness, Dale lifted my face to meet his eyes again. "You've seen one before, right?"

My eyes blinked wide at his cheeky grin. Of course, I'd seen a dick before. Even if I hadn't seen Malcolm's, I'd seen Dale's last night, in my kitchen. The memory of last night came flooding back, and I felt my entire body heat all over.

"I'm clean!" All but throwing myself from the shower, I snatched a towel from the rack and wrapping it around me. At the bed, I stared down at my underwear and dress. What was wrong with me? Getting naked with a virtual stranger and showering with him.

"Vera?" Dale came up behind me but didn't touch me. "Is everything alright?"

"I'd like to get dressed in private, please?"

Raising a brow, Dale looked around. The sarcasm of that look wasn't lost on me as he all but pointed out there was no private space in the room.

Biting my lip, my eyes went to the door, forcing myself to breathe his scent and calm down. "Please, Dale? I just need a moment to compose myself."

Tucking his towel tight around his waist, Dale nodded, his eyes tender as he stepped out of the cabin. Exhaling dramatically, I dressed then opened the door for Dale. "Thank you. I'll wait above."

Bowing his head, Dale closed the door. There wasn't an ounce of anger coming from him, nothing harmful about my reaction. If anything, Dale seemed ashamed. Understanding the feeling of having done something wrong when you hadn't, I hated to do it to someone else.

Weighed down with guilt, I trudged upstairs and sunk onto the lounge next to Jeremy. Taking one look at me, Jeremy put his arm around my shoulder, lowering his mouth to my ear. "Don't look so forlorn. You've done nothing wrong. He knows you need time, and he'll give you what you need." Picking up a bottle of water, he took a mouthful.

"Oh, cause I think I need mind-blowing sex. Knowing that comes with a commitment of marriage is rather daunting."

Jeremy spat his drink all over himself.

CHAPTER 15

*L*unch was at a little port town further down the coast. We walked into the seaside village, everyone hand-in-hand with their date. Stopping at a seafood restaurant, we ate our lunch out on the deck overlooking the sea. After our meal, we continued into the village to shop at some of the little shops.

Before heading back to the boat, Bob dragged us all to a little family-run Dutch ice creamery. Heidi and Juliet refused to eat any when the salesman offered them to sample a few flavors. I wasn't so restrained. After testing my fourth flavor, and moaning at how nice it tasted, I ordered a double scoop in a waffle cone. Turning around, I found everyone smirking at me. "What?"

"Like ice cream, do you?" Jeremy teased with a waggle of his brow.

My face grew warm. "It's a very nice ice cream."

"Damn, straight it is." Throwing his arm over my shoulders without warning, Bob tried to pull me into his side. Jolting, I winced, dropping my cone. Moving quickly, Dale caught it.

"Shit, sorry, Vera." Removing his arm, Bob pouted and cursed under his breath.

"It wasn't your fault. I'm sorry, it's a habit after this long."

With a nod, Bob moved away to take Juliet's hand. Offering me back my ice cream, Dale focused his eyes on mine. It took me a moment to realize I was about to cry, and that's why everyone was now avoiding looking at me.

Ignoring the ice cream, I stepped into Dale. Wrapping my arms around him, I buried my face against his chest and breathed. His earthy scent filled my nose, my lungs, then diffused into my system. My heartbeat slowed, and my tears evaporated.

Shifting his stance, Dale pressed both his strong hands into my back, firm, and reassuring. By the time I stepped back from him a minute later, the others were outside. Even the sales assistant was at the far end of the store, his back to us as if we needed the privacy.

Swallowing with discomfort at the public meltdown, I looked around. "Um, what happened to my ice cream?"

"Jeremy took it." Dale glanced outside where Jeremy was finishing off my cone. "I'll get you a new one." Lips brushing my brow, Dale tucked my hair behind my ear.

"Thank you for holding me." In case he thought I cared about the ice cream more than what his scent did for me.

Stroking my cheek, Dale gave me a gentle smile. Stepping up to the counter, he ordered my ice cream again, before ordering his own. When the clerk handed us our cones, he also gave Dale a bag with several tubs in it, I raised a brow at the bag.

"Whenever we come here, we stock up on our favorites for home. I got you a tub as well." He grinned at the smile on my face.

"Dale, don't get me used to you spoiling me if it's going to stop once you have me."

Dale's smile faltered. Caressing my cheek, he brushed his mouth across mine. My breath rushed out of me; my head dizzy. Staring into my eyes, his were focused and intent. "Vera, I already have you, so get used to me spoiling you. I haven't even started yet."

"You haven't?" Could he spoil me more than he had already today?

"Oh, no." Dale shook his head, his eyes darkening. "Just you wait until you allow me to fill your body."

The desire to be in Dale's arms naked destabilized me until I felt boneless and limp. In my head, I saw me screaming my pleasure as he filled me, and I collapsed sated to his chest.

"Then, I will give you whatever you need. And, if your prediction from our bonding proves true, you will never want for anything ever again."

Staring up at him awed, a switch clicked, and I frowned. "What prediction?"

Dale's eyebrows lifted, his eyes lightened as he straightened. "You don't remember?" Leading me out of the shop, Dale frowned when I shook my head. "What do you remember?"

"You bit me, it felt wonderful, and then I fell asleep. Why, did something else happen?"

Considering me, after a moment, Dale relaxed. "You murmured something, but I won't ruin the surprise if you can't remember."

Opening my mouth to object, Heidi cut me off.

"Do you know how much fat there was in ice cream? If I don't want to bloat before my shoot next week, I can't touch a lick of it."

Brows low over his eyes, Jeremy seemed unimpressed by her attitude. I couldn't help but notice Heidi was eyeing me and my ice cream the entire time she ranted.

Wrapping his arm around my waist, Dale slowed our walk, so we weren't within hearing of the others. "Jeremy can't stand it when women go on about their figures, or if they criticize another woman. Don't expect Heidi to be joining us on our outings anymore."

"Why not?"

"Because I know that look on Jeremy's face. He'll be shaking her free this evening." Considering something, Dale smirked. "Or tomorrow morning."

"Wait, so he knows he's going to break up with her, but will let it go for another night so he can get laid one last time?"

"I dare say it will be more than once." He put his mouth to my ear. "The girls usually leave walking funny on Sunday's. We like to get as much as we can when we can, even if that means very little sleep."

Eyes wide, I tripped remembering how often Dale and his ex-wife had sex in the vision he showed me. "So, being a hundred years old hasn't dampened your sex drive?"

Dale's laughter was silk on naked skin. "Goddess, no! Twenty-first-century women are the freest since pre-Christian times. We would be idiots to not enjoy the freedom from oppression that women have fought long and hard for. I'm a suffragette. Give women more rights and confidence to be the sexual beasts men fear. All the better for the men who don't suffer ego issues."

Doubtful of Dale's statement, I lifted a brow. "You don't have an ego?"

"Of course, I do. Every man does, but I'm secure enough to know that I don't have to beat a woman down to make me feel better. Men have been doing that for thousands of years because they feel it's the only way to have power over a woman. But oppressing women isn't the answer. Mistreating women doesn't make you a man, it just high-lights an inferiority complex."

Raising a brow at his jovial passion, I tilted my head assessing him. "Feel strongly about this, do you?"

"Don't you?"

"But no one has ever raped or beaten you, so we care about this for different reasons."

"I had a mother, Vera. My father never harmed her, but her father..." Dale drifted off. "I've lived for a long time. I lived through a time when women and children were possessions. As long as you didn't kill them, you could beat them or do whatever you wanted with them. I've watched spirited girls lose the light in their eyes as pathetic excuses for men broke them. All in the guise of protecting them or family pride."

We took a few steps in silence with Dale's eyes focused ahead. "When I became strong enough to draw my pack-mates to me, I made it clear; in this pack, we adore and cherish women. They are never harmed." Glancing ahead to Jeremy, Dale shrugged. "Yes, we enter casual liaisons. When Jeremy ends it, he will make it about him, and their age difference. Or he will be honest and say she needs more maturity before it could work. He won't be mean or an asshole about it. I've seen him do it in a way that the girl thinks she's the one ending the relationship."

Watching ahead, I could see Jeremy having the capability of ending things well. "Juliet seems lovely. She said she and Bob have been on and off over the last four years?"

"Juliet came from a bad home. Whenever things get serious between them, she panics and ends it. The first few times, it hurt Bob, now he takes it as a turn in the season. They've agreed to be in a relaxed relationship. They see other people, but it's never serious."

Watching how Bob let Juliet sneak a few licks of his ice cream when Heidi wasn't looking, my stomach warmed. "Do you think they'll make it?"

Dale gave my waist a squeeze. "I would wish for any of my pack to find the happiness of love and family."

Happiness flooded my system, but there was a little sadness too. Malcolm and my father stole twelve years of life, of love, of belonging to this pack. Learning about my own people was fascinating, I wanted to know more, and yet, I hesitated to ask. Trepidation of knowing why we were different from humans. The dread of finding out things that would haunt me, about myself and these men I was starting to like. Fear that someone would take it all away. So, I stayed quiet and let my questions build in my head, slotting clues together.

Returning to the yacht, we set sail home. Already exposed to more sun than I had in my entire life, I stayed in the inside. Sitting by me, Dale talked with the others. Every now and then, he tried drawing me in on the conversation, but I was happy to answer and return to listening. Arriving back at the port in the late afternoon, we disembarked towards the carpark.

"Why don't we get dinner here?" Jeremy suggested. "Saves me cooking when we get back."

"Sounds good to us." Bob smiled.

"We'll pass. Vera already had something out for dinner."

Dale's answer serving as a reminder that I'd offered to cook for him tonight. The others decided to stay for dinner, so we waved goodbye, and Dale drove me home.

"I'll duck home and get changed, then come down for dinner, if that's okay?" Dale checked as he pulled up out the front of my place.

"That would be good actually. Will give me time to get it on and have a moment to myself." Stepping out of the car, I let myself in as Dale drove his car up the drive to his place. Locking the door behind me, I set my bag from the sailing trip in my room. Rushing into the kitchen, I spent fifteen minutes getting dinner started.

In my bathroom, I frowned that my skin was a little pink. Stripping, I showered before rubbing aloe in and dressed in a fresh set of clothes. When I came into the lounge room, Dale was standing on the back porch looking over the yard. Opening the door, I watched as he walked in with a black gift box.

"This is for you. I meant to give it to you for the last week, but it wasn't the right time."

Frowning, I accepted the box and locked the door again. Placing the box on the coffee table, I opened it. Inside was the stunning and expensive robe I'd seen at the lingerie store. Glancing up at Dale, I was speechless.

"Jeremy saw you admiring it. He called me, and I asked him to pick it up for me to give to you." Taking the seat opposite me, Dale observed the way I fingered the black satin. "It's to replace the one I destroyed."

"Dale, it's beautiful, thank you." Standing up, I took the box into my room.

While I prepared dinner, Dale sat at the kitchen bench. He asked about my love of cooking, discussed specific recipes with me, and then told me more about his hobbies. After dinner, Dale helped me clean up. "Thank you for a fantastic meal." Dale held my hand as I walked him to the door. "Could I see you tomorrow?"

"I need to run in the morning, but I'm free afterward."

"That's right, Jeremy mentioned bringing you up to the gym and teaching you a few moves. How about we have lunch together?"

"Sounds doable."

Smiling, Dale kissed me on the cheek. "Goodnight, Vera. I'll see you tomorrow." Brushing his lips across mine as he pulled back, Dale stepped outside. Waiting for me to lock the door, he walked to the path.

It was an early departure, and I wondered why he didn't even try for more of a kiss. An hour later, the howls sounded up at the main house, and I understood, Dale had responsibilities. Kissing me would have led to a delay, and we didn't need a repeat of last night.

Thinking about last night, or today in the shower, made me squirm. Turning off the lights, I retreated to my bedroom. It's about time I found out how that toy the sales assistant at the lingerie store talked me into worked.

CHAPTER 16

"*Y*ou okay?" Jeremy stood above me as I coughed and rolled to the side.

Feet entered my peripheral, then Bob's voice scratched my ears like a bad itch. "Isn't she meant to be learning to defend herself, not getting thrown around like a rag doll?"

"All part of the process." Offering me his hand, Jeremy tilted his head, assessing me. When I stuck my finger in my ear and tried to get rid of the unhappy itch, Jeremy sighed. "It's okay, Vera. None of us like to see you mistreated, so even though Bob knows I'm training you, he can't help but get defensive."

Peering at Jeremy, I didn't understand the consoling tone he used. Maybe I'd flinched, and he worried I was going to spook.

Exhaling hard, Bob shifted his feet. "Well, Dale is waiting for you when you're ready, Vera."

Blinking at Bob, I was glad the itch had let up finally. "We agreed on lunch?"

"It's already eleven. You two have been at this for three hours."

Checking his watch, Jeremy lifted his eyebrows. "So it is. Okay, Vera, I want you to practice what we did this morning. We can have another session after I do the shopping on Wednesday." Nodding, I sat down to put on my joggers. "You got enough energy for the run home?"

"Yes, I'll be fine." Absentmindedly, I scratched my scar on my side. It tended to niggle after exercise.

Observing me, Jeremy clenched his jaw, and the sound of an angry hive of wasps filled my head.

Sighing, I stood up. "I stabbed him with a smashed bottle before he did this. It was self-defense on his part. He'd never cut me up before."

"Don't ever defend him, Vera. He should never have had you for you to get desperate enough to attack him."

Swallowing, I stared at the floor, trying to stop my eyes from filling with tears or retreating. The last was easier. Years of learning not to run or backstep from Malcolm. Still, survival instinct could undo any amount of resilience you tried to have.

When Jeremy snarled, I flinched, that made him scowl harder. "Fuck, I hate this! I'm sorry, Vera, I'll go calm down." Storming out of the room, Jeremy punched the wall on the way through.

The door slammed shut, I flinched again. Peering through my brows at the door, I found Bob standing with his back to me as if he'd stepped between Jeremy and me.

Bob turned his chin to his shoulder. "Grab your shoes, Vera, I'll see you out." His voice was terse as if he too were on edge. Shoving my feet into my shoes, I followed Bob out to the driveway.

We passed Howard on the way, he glared at me and all but spat at me. When he glared at me, I whimpered. "Oh my god, you're so weak and pathetic!" Howard launched at me. Backing into the wall behind me, I avoided his attack.

Grabbing Howard around the throat, Bob slammed him into the wall opposite me. "Go, Vera!"

Not needing him to tell me twice, I ran out of the house, down the drive, and then the length of the driveway to my cottage. Inside, I locked all the doors before crawling into my wardrobe and huddling into a tight ball. My heart was racing, and body trembling like I was outside in a snow storm. Any minute now, Malcolm would come through the door, drag me from my hide, and beat me unconscious.

This amount of fear wasn't healthy, but I'd had fourteen years of living on adrenalin. My heart jumped into my throat when two black boots below denim jeans stepped into the doorway. The owner inhaled, exhaled with a sigh, then they squatted down to peer into the wardrobe.

"Vera?" The plump lips below indigo eyes called a foreign name. "Vera, breathe, honey. Recognize where you are, who I am, that you're safe."

Those eyes were so gentle, so calm. They begged me to trust them. Something about them soothed me like his hands were rubbing down my back. Taking a deep breath, his scent intoxicated me, relaxed me, and without a doubt, I knew he'd protect me.

Crawling forward, I burrowed in against his chest. "Dale!"

Wrapping his arms around me, Dale put his nose into my hair and inhaled. "How am I meant to leave for the city tonight with you in this state?"

The idea of Dale leaving made me cling to him. Goddess, I didn't want to alone here with Howard next door. I didn't want Dale to let me go.

"Come with me? You can stay in my apartment, go shopping, we can go out to dinner, or you can cook for Jeremy and me." Dale waited for a few breaths. "Think about it. The idea of leaving you alone here kills me."

"Howard scares me. I don't trust him."

With his body rigid, Dale tightened his grip. The oxygen levels dropped, and his anger heated the air around us; but staying low, like a warm fire on a winter's night.

Whimpering, I snuggled tighter to him. Holding my head to his chest, Dale stuck his nose in my hair. "I know." We stayed like that for several more minutes, until Dale's phone ringing made him pull away. "Have a shower and get dressed. We'll leave as soon as you're ready."

After Dale left the room, it took me a few minutes to take stock of my surroundings and assure myself I was safe. Still shaking a little, I made my way into the shower. It wasn't until I poured the shampoo in my hand to wash my hair that I realized I was still dressed, sneakers, and all.

"...YOU don't cover for him, and you sure as hell tell me when he pulls that shit." Dale's angry voice greeted me outside my bedroom. Walking down the hall to the kitchen, I found Dale standing out on the back porch, growling into his phone. Noticing me, Dale took a breath to calm down and indicated he'd be a second.

"I understand that, but he needs to get himself under control." Dale looked at his watch. "You do that. I'm about to head out to my lunch date. We can discuss this when I get back." Hanging up the phone, Dale took a deep breath, then stepped back inside. "Sorry, are you ready?"

"How do you keep getting into my house?"

Looking sheepish, Dale shrunk into his shoulders as he lifted a key out of his pocket. "My former employee gave me a copy, in case he failed to turn up to work one morning." When I raised a brow at him, Dale shook his head and returned the key to his pocket. "If I hadn't had this, I wouldn't have been able to get in and help you when the goddess warned you of imminent danger."

"I... I don't like... I mean, I don't feel safe." It was a struggle to express my emotions on this. Could Howard access that key? What about the others? Dale having it actually didn't bother me. Was that right? Shouldn't it bother me?

Dale frowned as if watching every one of my thoughts cross my face. "Come stay with me in the city."

"I'm not good with crowds."

"You would be safe, Vera. My apartment is more secure than this place ever could be."

"Dale, I need to learn to do this. I need to take care of myself."

Taking my hand, Dale pleaded with his eyes. "For this week, Vera. Come stay with me for two days. Jeremy will bring you back Tuesday night. Then you can choose to stay with me or not for the rest of the week. Please?"

My gut twisted at the idea of saying no to him. "Can I have the day to think about it?"

Stepping in, Dale captured my lips in a gentle one-pinch kiss. "Of course. That you will consider it is enough."

Swooning, a little, I shook my head and took a step back. "You're turning me into one of those girls, aren't you?"

"No, Vera. You already were one of those girls, you've just hidden it under your defenses all these years."

"I disagree. Only you have ever made me feel light-headed with one kiss."

Dale's eyes glinted with mischief. "Imagine how you could feel with my lips all over you?"

Meeting his mischievous look with one of my own, I grinned. "I don't have to. I still have Friday night clear in my head. A kitchen has never turned me on so much, but every time I walk into mine now, I can only think of you."

Dale's eyes drifted to my kitchen bench. Groaning, he closed his eyes before looking back at me. "I believe it has the same effect on me. Let's go, before I convince you of a rematch."

Smirking, I grabbed my handbag. Dale took us out the back door, locking it as we left. We walked to his place via the forest path, collected his car, and headed out.

An hour later, a waiter led us to a table in a garden restaurant. As we approached a table with four men and one woman, Dale put his mouth to my ear. "We are having lunch with some friends I need you to meet."

"Dale," one of the men stood to greet us.

"Ralph, this is Vera."

Observing me over, Ralph had a broad smile on his face. His eyes touched my neck where Dale marked me, and his smile grew as he offered me his hand. "It's lovely to finally meet you, Vera."

"Finally?"

"Yes, Dale told us about you when Cameron met you. We planned to introduce ourselves and then our packs. But when Dale claimed you as his, we still asked to meet you."

My mouth went dry. "You're...?"

"Lycan's? Yes. We are the Liderii or the leaders of our people." Ralph turned sweeping his hand across the table waiting behind him. "If your pack followed tradition, we should have met when you were a child." He indicated the only woman at the table. "Cerese should have been your tutor in all things Lycan. Please join us." Stepping back to stand by his seat, Ralph introduced me to the others.

Standing by me, Dale placed his hand in the middle of my back. Then, when we sat, he set my hand on his thigh under the table and covered it with his hand.

It turned out, Dale was one of the Liderii. When Cameron told him I was an unmated female Lycan, Dale contacted the Liderii to report finding me. They decided Dale should let me move in, befriend me, and find out why the how and why of me.

Of course, when Dale met me himself, Alpha had been in control, so that hadn't been the best start. Everything Dale learned about my abuse and issues he'd passed on too. When Dale realized I was his mate, he'd notified the Liderii immediately.

"You couldn't have found a better alpha as your mate, Vera," Cerese assured me. All the other alphas at the table bristled, especially Ralph, who was Cerese's mate. "Oh, shush. We all know Dale is the sweet-heart of the Liderii." Squeezing Ralph's hand, Cerese winked at Dale.

"You're full-blood, like me?"

"Yes. The only other. Though, now that we know what happened to you, we are wondering if there are any others?"

"Considering we make our packs implode, it shouldn't be hard to find any others."

Everyone sort of went into slow motion, as if any sudden move-ments might set me off. It was Cerese who cleared her throat. "A good starting point indeed, Vera, but one that is already years beyond when a girl should meet her mate. Your mother wasn't human, yet we have no record of who she was, so like with you, we weren't notified of her existence."

"Unless, of course, my mother had never known she was anything but human?"

Everyone at the table frowned. "Was that the case?" Ralph enquired.

"I have no idea. I don't remember anything about her. She wasn't in my life for as long as I can remember." You can't miss what you never had if you never knew you should have it.

Again, the table fell quiet. This time, the arrival of our food broke the awkwardness. We started eating, and Dale made the subject light, discussing their packs. I learned a lot during that meal.

Ralph was already fifty when he mated with Cerese on her sixteenth birthday. They'd met and recognized each other as mates the year prior. Cerese was sixty, but she didn't look a day over twenty-five. Cerese couldn't shift, nor had she fallen pregnant. Even with the human methods of ovulation kits, she couldn't conceive.

"When you mated, did you have a vision of your life ahead with Ralph?"

Cerese tilted her head appraising Dale and his question. "It was so long ago."

"Have you ever dreamed real?" I butted in.

Blinking, Cerese glanced at all the others. "Ah, no. Do you?"

"Since I was a child."

"Vera only found out she was one of us after one of her dreams left her injured. She needed me to seek medical attention for her." Dale then continued to describe the nature of my dream, Malcolm, and what he did to me. While the rest of the table sat looking pale and appalled. "When I sank fang to mark her, Vera whispered a preview of our future together. I wasn't sure if that was the norm or a part of her gift."

The entire table fell quiet when Quinton, the oldest and most silent spoke. "We had a female, long ago, to whom the goddess spoke in her dreams. She was quite different from the females we get now. Her mate and she were very happy together. When her mate died, she started dreaming of the deaths of her pack. She would wake injured." Quinton fell quiet.

"It killed her, didn't it?" Already knowing the answer, my eyes filled with tears.

"No one heeded her. Only one listened to her. The dreams claimed the woman before the hunters came and annihilated their pack. But the one who listened survived."

"There are hunters?"

Quinton lifted his grey bushy brows over his aged, grey, eyes. "They were witch hunters. In that age, everything different was a witch, and killed as such." He stroked his grey beard. "Perhaps, you are a descendant of her child who escaped. Perhaps, you are she again?"

CHAPTER 17

$\mathcal{T}$he ride home was quiet. The myth sparked a debate at our lunch table over the belief of reincarnation. Saying no more, Quinton let the others argue all the reasons I couldn't be a reincarnation. Instead, he studied me. I was glad to fade into the background with Quinton and Dale, who also stayed out of the argument. In fact, other than farewells, Dale hadn't said another word.

When we pulled up out the front of my place, I chose to share my thoughts. "I don't believe in past lives."

Killing the engine, Dale sat back, his eyes focused out of the windscreen. "The woman Quinton spoke of; she's known to all Lycan's. Luna is what they call her, but no one remembers her true name. She wasn't born human, but a wolf. She was beautiful but endured a horrible life."

Licking his lips, Dale gripped the steering wheel. "Abandoned by her mother, her sire unknown, humans raised her. She struggled to fit in with humans, her temper, not what a woman's should be in those days. The restriction of clothes, of being in bed at night instead of roaming the woods, was all very abrasive. As a young woman, her beauty attracted a wealthy man's interest, and he married her. After that, she suffered repeated beatings and rapes by her husband."

Dale didn't look at me while he related this story, and I felt like he was telling my life. Tears streamed down my face like a waterfall of pain.

"One day, when the violence led to the loss of her unborn child, Luna shifted into her wolf. It was a form she'd forgotten after her abandonment. She ripped her husband's throat out and left the human world behind. It was years later, she met her mate in wolf form, and in wolf form, they mated. She bore him five cubs, three boys, and two girls, all in the same litter. Remaining wolf until her young shifted the first time, Luna also changed and joined her mate and his pack. While she was with him, until the day he died, Luna lived a good and happy life." Dale shifted, taking my hand in his. "It was like the fates hated her, and the love of her mate protected her."

Observing my tears, Dale didn't reach out to touch me in any other way. He sat there and watched my tears fall and that I didn't try to hide them from him.

"I don't believe in past lives. I do believe history repeats itself until we learn from past mistakes."

Frowning, Dale gripped my chin between his thumb and forefinger. "You are not a mistake, Vera. What happened to you, the men in your pack, allowing that to happen to you, that was the mistake." When I looked away, Dale sighed. "The similarity between you may have nothing to do with the circumstances of your birth. The Goddess may have chosen you for the strength of your soul. The Goddess watches her children. Those that survive so much horror with their souls still intact, she might give the blessing of sight too?"

"Dale, you missed the point of Quinton's comparison. Those dreams that the Goddess' blessed' Luna with, caused her untold agony, and killed her. Just like my dream could have killed me the other night."

"No, Vera, you missed the point. The hunters who killed Luna's pack and all but one of her children were witch hunters. They didn't sweep through the packhouse with a machine gun and kill everyone where they stood. They captured them, tortured them for days on end, brutalized them, then killed them to save their soul. It was a well-documented event, the torturing of the body to save the soul. Luna escaped the horror inflicted on her pack. The Goddess allowed her to warn her pack, then took her to save her the worst of it."

Panic rose in my breast bone, my heart thudding against my chest. "He's going to find me, isn't he? That's what she's trying to tell me?"

Giving me the saddest eyes, I'd ever seen on him, Dale looked defeated already. Throwing open the car door, I ran for the house. Struggling to unlock the door, I sobbed as I nearly broke the key in the lock.

Soothing and calm, Dale reached around me, pulling my body back against his. One of his hands pressed on my abdomen, which somehow pushed my panic out of me like an exhalation. His other hand took my trembling fingers with the key and guided it into the lock, helping to open the door.

"You are my mate now, Vera. Those people you met today, if Malcolm dares try to take you from me, they will bring every pack in our country down on him. You belong to me now, there is nothing he can do about that."

Kissing over my shoulder, Dale stepped us inside as he moved my cardigan aside.

"You don't own me; not completely."

"Not yet."

Tilting my face so I could see him in my peripheral vision, Dale touched my cheek. Turning my head a little bit more to capture my lips. One kiss, a second longer one, the third his tongue flitted against my lips. Shifting his stance, Dale swiveled my body to face him and moved us against the wall, pressing his body into mine.

Already tingling from his touch, my nerves burst to life. Nothing had ever felt this good, and I didn't want it to stop. Every sensory perception was firing, absorbing sights, sounds, smells, and touch. Dale's caress was sunlight after months of snow. It melted my body to his, warmed me to my core, made me want to stretch out, so he had more of me to feel. When Dale found the parts he wanted to inspect covered, he removed the barrier.

The first rip of material startled me. Blinking down as Dale dropped his mouth to my exposed breast, I gulped. An inferno roared through the center of my body, melted my womb, and my knickers grew damp.

Freeing my skin from the confines of my clothing, Dale explored each exposed surface. Pressing my shoulders into the wall, I rocked my hips forward. His tongue sought my slit, licking and sucking at my bud to encourage me to open for him.

When my hand grasped a fistful of his hair and tugged hard, Dale released his grip on my hips and stood. Kicking off his shoes the same moment he pulled his shirt over his head. My hands reached out to touch his chest, trace the muscles of his torso. Freezing lowering his fly, Dale closed his eyes and exhaled roughly at my touch. His eyes opened lazily, lust-filled indigo met mine and frowned. Shaking his head, Dale stepped out of my reach.

"When we mate the first time, I want your green eyes looking back at me, not the mask you hide behind. The eyes are the window to the soul, Vera. They tell you everything you need to know about a person. When I'm with you, I want to see the real you."

Blinking, still stunned by the sudden end of his attention, it took me a moment to understand.

Grabbing his shirt from the ground, Dale secured his pants and started for the door. "Pack a bag for a few nights. I'll be back in an hour to pick you up."

"Dale, I didn't agree to go to the city." Collecting my shredded dress, I held it in front of me like a shield.

"Howard is staying here this week. Do you want to be here alone with him next door?" When I turned my head away ashamed, Dale shoved open the door. "I thought so. Be ready in an hour."

"I didn't start this. Don't get shitty at me because you stopped."

Coming back through the door, Dale threw his shirt to the side and kissed me furiously. Swaying into his embrace, I moaned at the depth of emotion in that kiss. When he pulled back, Dale leaned his forehead to mine while I tried to catch my breath.

"I stopped because you're not ready, Vera. Your body is willing, but your eyes showed your fear. I don't want to make love to you while you tremble like a rabbit who knows its doom. I want you to want me, as much as I want you. Heart and soul." Deflating in his arms, I knew he was right. Kissing my nose, Dale stepped away. "I'll see you in an hour."

Precisely an hour later, I was sitting with a small bag on my front porch when Dale pulled up. Despite walking to the car by the time he got out, Dale still walked around to open the door for me. Instead of sitting immediately, I stood and waited for Dale to meet my eyes. When he did, his eyes lit up.

"No more hiding. Malcolm knows I'm alive, Auburn hair and brown eyes aren't going to fool him."

Gripping the back of my neck in one large hand, Dale pulled me into a deep kiss before lowering me into the car. He didn't say a word. Closing my door, Dale took his seat and put the car in drive.

Waiting until we were on the freeway, I crossed my fingers and hoped Dale agreed. I'd wanted this since I found out it was a thing. "I have a term before we mate."

Dale glanced at me, intrigued. "Okay?"

"I want to get married. I want the pretty dress, the ceremony, the dancing. I want our first night to be our wedding night."

Grin splitting his face, Dale laughed. "Told you, you were one of those girls."

CHAPTER 18

*I*t was dark when we arrived in the city. Dale touching my shoulder to wake me since I'd fallen asleep halfway there. "We're here."

Helping me out of the car, Dale walked me to the elevator nearby. We parked in an underground car park, so there was nothing to tell me where we were. Taking the elevator to the second top floor, we stepped out into a grey marble hallway. Placing his hand into the small of my back, Dale led me towards the door on the right, unlocking it and letting me inside. Once we were inside, Dale turned on the lights. I marveled at the sumptuous furnishings of his open-plan apartment. The color scheme was all various shades of grey, black, silver, and white.

Around the kitchen and lounge room were a bank of windows providing a view of the city lights outside. Opening the door to the balcony, I stepped out to enjoy the night air. Inside, Dale started talking to someone on the phone in the kitchen. Calming my para-noid mind, I focused my attention back on the view. Dale's warmth pressed against my back, inciting tingles to spark all over my body.

"Dinner will be here in thirty minutes." His hand sliding down my arm to take my hand and lead me back inside. "Let me show you around." Opening the only other door in the apartment, Dale stepped us into a bedroom. The room had a large bed and open plan bathroom, separated by the deep bathtub. "This is our bedroom."

"Our?"

"Yes, I only have one bedroom. We can share a bed without anything happening, Vera." Dale placed a kiss before my ear; I shivered.

"Are you sure? We can't even share a kitchen without nearly..."

Dale moved his body closer. "I want you, Vera, but you have to want me too."

Closing my eyes, I imagined all the ways I could let him have me. His scent intoxicating me, drawing me into a waking version of the dream of intimacy with him. The warmth of Dale's skin disappeared from mine. Opening my eyes, I stood in the room alone. Blinking, I looked around. "Dale?"

"In the lounge room."

As I moved back out to the lounge room, Dale looked up from his computer and checked the time. "Twenty minutes. I hope I last longer than that when we actually do mate the first time."

My cheeks caught fire. "You knew what I was...?"

"The smile and moaning sort of gave it away. Your desire is growing stronger if you are having waking dreams of us." The satisfaction was smug on his face.

Covering my face with my hands, I groaned as the embarrassment radiated through me. A door chimed.

Rising, Dale opened the door and grabbed two papers bags from a delivery man, then came back to the kitchen. "I warned you the urge to mate would be powerful. Ever eat take out?"

Shaking my head, I moved towards the wonderful smell coming from the bags.

"Get ready for your first take out experience then." Opening the dishes along the bench, Dale handed me a plate and told me to take what I'd like.

Serving a spoon of everything onto my plate, I tried a bit of everything. Some of it was delicious, others not so much. Waiting while I dished myself more of what I liked, Dale then put the rest on a plate for himself. Stealing my plate, Dale made his way over to the lounge. "Come and eat."

We sat on the lounge eating. When I'd finished eating, I sat watching Dale. When he finished, he stood up and took my plate from me. "Want dessert?"

Following him to the Kitchen, I eyed the beautiful kitchen with eagerness. "Sure. Want me to make it?"

Grinning, Dale caught my waist and lifted me to the kitchen bench. "You already did." With a wicked grin, Dale pulled my pants from under me, leaving my bare bottom on the kitchen counter.

"Dale!"

Smirking with evil intent, Dale lifted my feet to his shoulders and ducked his face to nose my slit. Inhaling me, the air rushed past my moist skin as he breathed me. Griping the edge of the kitchen bench as his tongue tasted me, my eyes went wide. Biting my lip as Dale ate me in a way I'd never even imagined.

Foreplay had always been a few rubs and kisses, never this. My eyes rolled back in my head as Dale licked and sucked my clit and folds. Dale's tongue teased my entrance. The sensations eliciting moans, gasps, and other sounds from me that I'd never made before.

My legs were shaking, and I was whimpering in new pleasure when Dale pulled back to assess me. Gazing into my natural eyes, Dale blew across my trembling clit. My body thrashed about uncontrollably. Holding my hips tight, Dale buried his face again, licking and sucking my orgasm from me. He continued until the aftershocks of pleasure finished, leaving me limp and boneless.

Standing straight, Dale kissed my abdomen, then lifted my mouth to his. I could taste myself on his mouth, like apricot nectar. Kissing across to my ear, Dale used his hands in my hair to turn my head and tonged my ear lobe. "Best dessert I've ever eaten."

Voice rough from singing his praises, I gripped his shirt. "Dale, this better not be a dream."

Laughing, Dale scooped me up into his arms and carried me into bed. "Vera, this was just the start. You're in my bed for two nights, and I plan to have you gegging for it by Wednesday morning."

"Gegging?" I grunted when he dropped me on the bed.

Leaning over me, Dale lowered his body over mine. His erection pressing hard into my very sensitive areas. "To lust after something," Dale rocked his hips against me, and I bit my lip on a moan, "especially a desire to have sex."

"The sex isn't the problem. I'd do that now if it weren't for the commitment that comes with it."

Smoothing my hair from my face, Dale gazed into my eyes. "Sex is always a commitment of some sort for women. Don't let modern thinking fool you. You are letting someone inside you. Opening yourself to someone like that, it leaves you at your most vulnerable." Dale nipped his teeth along my jaw, and my nails dug into his triceps a little. "Sex is also power, Vera. You hold the power of my pleasure and your pleasure when we are together. I don't want to give you power over me unless I know you are in this for keeps?"

"Do I have any other choice?"

Looking hurt, Dale caressed my face. "You will always have a choice, Vera. You could have left; you could have refused to mate with me. True, had you made that choice, you would have found others and sent their pack insane. Now, that you know the outcome, that would have weighed on your conscience, but it was your choice."

Turning my face, I swiped away the tears that had started to fall.

"Not much choice, granted, but still a choice." Dale rubbed his face around my neck, scent-marking me. "You still could leave. It would hurt us both, but you could." Tensing suddenly, Dale lifted himself from me. "Damn it!"

The brown pushed out the indigo in his eyes, his wolf-gold trying to take over. Pulling back from him, I huddled against the bedhead wondering what happened.

Climbing from the bed, Dale put his back to me. "Alpha wants me to take you, to make you ours, to fill you with cubs and fuck you so hard you can't stand to walk, let alone leave. So, I'm going to go do a few laps in the pool to calm down. Get some sleep." Walking out, Dale left me there.

Swallowing hard, I remained still until the apartment door shut. Exhaling dynamically, I collected myself and my bag and changed into my pajamas. Tired after training with Jeremy, I climbed between Dale's bamboo sheets and went to sleep.

Vaguely aware of Dale climbing into bed, I took a deep breath and relaxed into him. Snuggling me to him, the dream of things he could do to me on a kitchen bench stole me away.

Waking with a smile in the morning, the sound of a man panting and the bed rocking a little greeted me. It took me a second to recognize the noise, then everything I had not to move or show I was awake.

Dale's pumping grew faster, his restrained moans climbing to a crescendo. "Goddess, Vera!"

Getting his breathing back under control, Dale rolled towards me, placing his mouth to my ear. "That was some dream, Sweet Pea." Kissing me quick, Dale moved out of the bed.

Watching him walk naked into the shower, I enjoyed the view from behind. Dale was such a delicious specimen; I wanted to eat him all up. The image of joining him in the shower and doing just that made me snicker.

"I felt that, naughty girl. Either put your mouth where your mind is or think of knitting. Some of us have to work, and a cold shower does not put me in a good mood."

Biting my lip, I rolled onto my back and touched my sensitive flesh. Everything was still tender from the tongue-lashing last night. Imagining Dale's mouth on me again, I gasped.

A groan sounded from the shower. "That's just mean!"

"You could always do it for me."

The bathroom fell quiet for a moment. The shower shut off and Dale didn't even bother drying as he walked back towards me still dripping wet. "You're asking for trouble, Sweet Pea."

Gesturing to the bed, I rose to my knees. "Lay down. Let me show you how naughty I can be."

Smirking, Dale laid on his back. Straddling his face, I licked down his torso until I reached his full and thick glory. "Nice recovery."

"That's you, Vera. Your desire will always call me to you."

Taking him in hand, I lowered my mouth as I sunk my hips down over his face. Best way to start the day.

CHAPTER 19

*T*here is something about men in suits. Yes, I've seen one or two that suits do not look good on, very few though. Dale in a suit, with his model looks, fit body, and the power he already exuded …it's the stuff of wet dreams.

"Are there gay Lycan's?"

Dale's eyebrows lifted over the newspaper at me. "Are you trying to tell me you think you're gay? Because you react to me pretty strongly."

Setting a Spanish omelet in front of him, I returned to the kitchen to serve up my breakfast. "You're my mate, I'd react to you even if I was gay. Also, I'm pretty sure you could make a few of the lesbians in the world move their orientation closer to bisexual."

Dale laughed. "There are a few. Alexia swings back and forth on occasion."

"The doctor is gay right?" Taking a sip of coffee, I flipped my omelet.

"How'd you know? Most don't pick it."

"He didn't react to me. Not that I'm egotistical, but he was touching me, close to me, and he didn't look at me the way straight men do." Plating up, I set the pan back on the stove to cool.

"He reacted to you, Vera, just not in a way familiar to you. Why do you think he was keen for us to mate?"

"Oh." Looking down at my meal, I remembered how determined I'd been not to mate with Dale. That hadn't even been a week ago. Lifting my eyes to Dale's, I wondered how I got so turned around.

Throwing back his chair, Dale stood. "Don't, Vera. Just don't."

Shaking my head, I started backing away. Striding towards me, Dale pulled me to him, kissing me passionately.

"Stop!"

Dale kissed me harder, deeper.

"Dale, please?"

Yanking away, anger rushed out from him like someone opening a hot oven door. Spinning away, Dale swiped his hand across the bench sending plates and coffee cups crashing to the floor, smashing on the porcelain tiles. Food and drink splattered everywhere.

Exhaling roughly, Dale leaned onto the kitchen bench. "Damn it! Don't put that wall back up, please? I am trying so hard to prove you can trust me. You don't understand what this is like for me. Our bond was instantaneous. My need for you has been overwhelming since the moment I caught your scent. It should have been the same for you. You're not a virgin, not a child, there was no reason we didn't mate immediately. When you fight your nature and fight our bond, I feel that physically, like a sore tooth in the back of my jaw. It's unbearable."

Standing straight, Dale wiped his hands over his face. He didn't turn to look at me, cowering in the corner, struggling to breathe through his frustration.

"I constantly feel like I'm dancing with you, Vera. Two steps forward, one step back. I can't keep this up forever. I came so close to losing control of my wolf last night. I want our mating to be something you want to do. Not just because I get you hot and bothered, but because you want to spend the rest of your life with me. Eventually, the wolf will win over if you keep backing away from me."

Taking a pained breath, Dale clenched his fists by his sides. "Especially when you whimper in the corner like you are doing now because my instinct is to protect you, Vera. To come over there and make love to you until you remember I'm your mate, and I'd never hurt you."

Leaving the kitchen, Dale grabbed his stuff and walking out the door. When the oxygen levels returned to normal, I crept forward and started cleaning up the floor. I cried the entire time I cleaned. Not because I feared Dale, because he was right. Every time I pushed Dale away, I was going against my instinct. I'd never felt more alive or happier than in his arms or in his presence. Dale made me feel whole, safe and loved. So, why was I fighting against my instincts? It's not like I'd ever experienced this with Malcolm, so I should be able to trust my instincts.

Sitting hard on the floor, I hugged myself as I rocked back and forth. Malcolm. He knew I was alive, and no doubt searching for me. Malcolm was the reason I wouldn't get my hopes up, or allow myself true happiness, for fear of having it taken all away.

Yet, Malcolm was the reason I should let this happen sooner rather than later. If I was with Dale, Malcolm couldn't touch me, he'd start a war trying. At the same time, I knew why that reason was holding me back also.

Getting up, I went to the bathroom and washed my face. Grabbing my phone, I called Jeremy. "I need your help with something."

"If it's mind-blowing sex, as much as I'd love to help you out, I have to pass," Jeremy teased.

"Close. I need a chaperone through this city."

"THAT WAS MORE fun than I expected. When Jeremy told me you needed someone to hold your hand, I worried I'd be taking you to the bank."

"Sorry to disappoint."

When Alexia first turned up at the apartment, she'd been anything but happy about being my escort. When I told her I needed to go dress shopping, she was full of beans. We'd spent most of the day out, had lunch together, shopped for a few other things together and sort of bonded.

We arrived at a floor, and Alexia led the way off the elevator. "Here to see the boss, Caprice," Alexia announced to the receptionist.

Caprice, a lithe blond in her late forties, didn't even look up. "He's in a meeting, on the next level. Can it wait?"

Alexia smirked at me and lowered her voice. "She doesn't know I'm Dale's daughter. She thinks Hymn and I are banging the boss because he just lets us walk in whenever we want."

Finally glancing up from her computer, Caprice finally noticed I was there. "Who's this? You know any newbies get vetted by the agents: take her down there."

"This is the bosses girlfriend, or actually, his fiancée, her name is Vera."

Mouth falling open, Caprice recovered a moment later. "Like he'd let you hang out with his fiancée. Get lost, Alexia. I'm not in the mood."

Rolling her eyes, Alexia took my arm and led me down the corridor. "Fine, don't believe me. Vera will wait in his office until he gets back."

"What?"

"Trust me, Mr. Hearn will be happy."

"No, wait!" Caprice tried to stand up to stop us, but got tangled in her phone headset and started cursing.

Hauling me through a glass door into a smaller office space, Alexia chuckled. "This is Jeremy's office." Shoving open the next door, Alexia came to a stop. "This is Dale's...oh, that's what she meant by next level up."

Dale was in his office, standing in front of a naked woman. This might have upset me, but there was also a naked man in front of a green screen. Standing with a camera in his hands, Jeremy watched as Dale gave the models directions.

"Alexia," Dale greeted his daughter without looking over at us. After adjusting something on the woman, Dale moved, allowing me to see Hymn and Adam were the naked models. When Dale indicated the shoot to continue, Jeremy nodded at me before lifting the camera.

That's when Dale saw me. He smiled brightly, frowned, and then looked at me waiting for me to let him know if he should be happy by my being here.

Smirking at me, Alexia shooed me forward.

Licking my lips, I moved forward to meet him. "Should I ask?"

Glancing over his shoulder, Dale sighed. The man was holding the woman, covering her breasts and pretending to bite her. "We do shoots for underground media too."

"Underground Media?"

As if on cue, the male forced the woman onto all fours before him. Staring wide-eyed, I watched as his body became hazy, like he was evaporating, and fell to the ground. A billow of charcoal smoke hung where his body was, then it sucked down into the form of a wolf.

Stepping forward, I stood mesmerized as the wolf mounted the girl from behind and licked up her spine. "Oh!"

In the pit of my stomach, I felt empty. You know that feeling you get when you go over a hill quickly, and your stomach drops out? That's what it felt like. Placing my hand over my abdomen, a waking dream swept over me.

In the yard behind my cottage, I was sunbaking on a towel. A shadow loomed over me. Opening my eyes, I smiled at alpha. He sniffed my crutch, and I laughed and tried to push his head away. When he licked up my stomach, I giggled with how ticklish I was. When he licked over my breasts, making the bikini wet with his slobber, I tried to cover myself.

'Dad, look at her eyes.'

Frowning, I looked around for Alexia.

'Shh,' Dale hushed from my other side.

Swinging my head to find him, I found myself alone in the yard. The sun had gone, and darkness was closing in, so was the cold. Rolling onto my stomach, I stood up, looking around the yard. My heart was pounding, my breath rasping. Something wasn't right.

Grabbing up the towel, I went to go back inside. Out of the corner of my eye, I saw a dark shape move in my vision. Stopping, I turned to look, but nothing was there, and yet, I knew something was here. Scanning the backyard as I moved back to the steps, I struggled to breathe through my fear.

Reaching the steps, I turned my attention to the cottage. I froze at what waited for me at the top of the steps.

"Did you really think you could get away from me, Viridia?" Malcolm took the steps down toward me. In his black suit, he looked good, his power emanating from him, but I'd met Dale now, Malcolm was a shadow on him.

Resisting screaming, I backed away. "You can't have me."

Moving faster than I could, Malcolm grabbed my hair in his fist and yanked me toward him. I whimpered, tears streaming down my face. Fear was suffocating my body. "You belong to me!" Hissing, Malcolm crushed his mouth to mine.

Screaming, I thrashed against him. Taking my bottom lip between his teeth, Malcolm bit down hard. Blood burst into my mouth, Malcolm moaned, so I returned the favor.

"Bitch!"

Pulling back, his lip still caught in my fangs, Malcolm swung and punched me in the face. Falling to the floor, lights burst in my vision. Pain swarmed my brain like wasps, blocking out the sound of my surroundings. Spitting out the piece of Malcolm's lip I'd taken with me, I blinked to stabilize my mind.

"Oh, you want to play rough, do you? Let's play rough then." When Malcolm paused, I looked up at him. He smiled down with his bleeding lip. "Vera."

"No!"

Swinging his leg, his foot caught me in the stomach, sending me flying across the room where I impacted with some furnishings and a wall. Crumpling to the tiled floor, I lay there crying.

"Vera?" Dale was beside me, rubbing my back. When I risked checking it was actually him, his eyes fastened on my bleeding lip. The gold pushing into the indigo and chocolate, Dale touched my chin, but then removed his hand. "How close is he?"

Alexia was standing right there behind him, her face pale with shock.

Spitting blood out of my mouth, onto his floor, I groaned in pain and slumped into his hold. "He knows my name."

Holding me, Dale moved me to the sofa to rest while the photo shoot finished. Using his resources, Dale tried to see where a search on my name could lead them.

My bond with Dale sped the healing process, so I could soon sit and watch the rest of the shoot take place. Moving to Jeremy's side, I observed the shots he took. Once he finished the publication shots, he asked me if I wanted a go. Instructing me on the basics, Jeremy let me have a play. Hymn and Adam hammed it up for me, Hymn even doing her partial shift and pretending to attack Adam.

"You've got a good eye, Vera." Concentrating on the shots I took, Jeremy looked across the room. "Alexia, join the party."

Squealing, Alexia jumped in with Adam and Hymn. They mocked out a threesome. About the time they forgot there was a camera in the room, I stopped photographing. Cheeks hot and feeling flustered, I handed the camera back to Jeremy.

Lifting a brow, Jeremy put it back in my hands. "Shoot it. Let's see how good that eye of yours is."

"I'm worried about it sucking me into a waking dream and him being there."

Combing a strand of hair away from my face, Jeremy met my eyes. "Are you going to stop sleeping, Vera?" I shook my head. "If the Goddess wants to find you, hiding in the waking world won't stop her."

Swallowing my dread, I turned the camera on the three writhing bodies on the floor. Dale left the room when the threesome stopped being play-acting but hadn't insisted I join him.

"Is this a normal thing for the twins and Adam?" I whispered to Jeremy.

He observed the trio. "We all get carried away at times, Vera. The girls have dated a few of the pack members, but they aren't mates, so it's not serious. If he got one of them pregnant, then that would change things, but it's highly unlikely."

Taking the camera back, Jeremy scrolled through the photos. "Once a month, we shoot the underground stuff. I've always been the photographer, but doing that puts me behind on my work. Want a job?"

"What, as the photographer?"

"You've got a good eye. It gets you out, earns you a good income, and in a way, introduces you to your own species a bit more." Hooking the camera up to the computer, Jeremy hit the button to download the pictures. "I'll run it past Dale, but I'm sure he'd jump at the chance to have you with him for a week straight each month."

Watching the three panting models on the floor, I bit my lip. "Is it always like this?"

"Everyone lost control with the pheromones you released during your initial daydream. Your fear dampened it, but not enough."

Biting my lip, I averted my gaze when my cheeks heated.

"Should I ask what you dreamed about?"

My cheeks caught fire.

"You know that's why Dale left the room?" Lifting the camera, Jeremy took a shot of me. "Your pheromones nearly made him lose control. Your fear and pain fueled his temper, followed by your arousal again; it got too much for him to control."

"Arousal?"

"Yes, Vera. Your arousal for what you saw. You were thinking about Dale and me with you."

Hiding my face behind my hands, my entire face and chest burned. "You could feel that?"

Glancing down at his crutch, Jeremy raised a brow in cheek. "Yes."

Shifting one finger, I observed the evidence of his desire and hid my face again.

Jeremy put his mouth to my ear. "If I were as horny as your mate, I'd have needed to leave too. Thankfully, I spent all weekend doing more than you were thinking about. So I could control myself a little better. Jeremy peered down again. "Still, I'm going to need to pick up tonight. Hope you're right to cook." Winking at me, Jeremy walked out.

"If you are going to start doing the shoots, we are going to need fuck breaks," Hymn chuckled across the room.

My entire body caught fire. That made everyone laugh a little more.

"Be more worried about Jeremy having those photos," Adam teased, pulling his pants on. "They may end up in the next edition."

"I'll kill him," Alexia threatened.

Hymn shrugged. "I want a copy. Those sort of photos keeps a girl warm at night."

Dressing, Alexia came over to me. "I'll take your dress back to the apartment for you. You need to talk to Dad." Collecting our shopping, Alexia herded the others out to give me a moment to myself.

When the door opened again, Dale held it open but didn't come inside. "Follow me, this room needs airing out."

CHAPTER 20

"*I* don't want to mate with you because I fear Malcolm."

Dale watched me from where he rested his bum on the board room table.

"I want to be with you. Goddess, I want to be with you so badly, but I can't help it. Yes, my instincts tell me you're safe to be with, and that I can trust you. Believe me, I've shown an enormous amount of trust in you already." I fidgeted with the hem of my dress. "You did in-prison me in the cottage instead of telling me why I shouldn't leave. I was so angry at you for that. Then you turn up, sink your fangs in me, and hey, I'm all giddy and girly for you. It scares me."

Gritting his teeth, Dale studied me. "Are you asking me to let you go, Vera?"

"No."

"Are you asking me to give you more time? Space, maybe?"

"Would that do any good?"

"Probably not."

"I asked for something to happen before we mated. I bought the dress today. As soon as you can organize the ceremony, it can happen."

When Dale's face relaxed, his pupils dilating, and his mouth hinting at a smile, I sighed. The man was beautiful. Everything about him. Not only was he gorgeous to look at, but his personality was kind and pleasant. Having years of exposure to assholes, I knew a good man when I saw him. Several times now, Dale lost his temper near me and didn't harm me, or even suggest that it was a consideration to hit me. He was my mate, and he deserved me trying to make this work. Still, there were limits to my readiness for moving forward.

"I'm not moving into the house with you yet. When you are home, you can stay with me, and I'll stay one night at the weekend in your bed."

Considering my restriction, Dale pursed his lips. "We can do that for a while, but I'd like you to consider traveling to the city with me, staying here the nights I'm here."

"Possible. I want to do the cooking. Jeremy is good, I'm sure, but I love cooking for people, so I'd love to cook for the pack on the weekends."

"I can't see anyone taking issue with that, Vera." Standing straight, Dale shoved his hands in his pockets. "Are they your only conditions?"

"There's one more," I advised stepping towards him.

"Not to close, Vera. Only if you're going to allow me to pound you into this table."

The visual combining with the ghost of his touch made me moan. "Dale…" The daydream swept me away before I could stop it. Kissing, touching, our clothes strewn to the floor. The table was cold under my breasts as Dale bent me over it and shoved into me.

"Vera!" Breaking me from the daydream, I was wheezing, Dale was panting. "Can I fuck you?"

Yes, yes, please, yes. "Not…"

Moving faster than I could track to the door, Dale shoved it open. "I'll see you at the apartment after work."

Sinking into the chair at the table, I hung my head. It was getting ridiculous. You couldn't mention sex around me without the bond sucking me into a waking wet dream.

When I left the meeting room, Jeremy was waiting. "Do you know how to get back to the apartment?"

"No."

"Didn't think so. Let's go before you make the whole place horny. You're giving off pheromones like you're in heat."

Busying myself cooking all afternoon, I tried not to think about the happenings of the day. Dale was getting a three-course meal, but if he didn't come home soon, I'd add another course to the menu.

Glancing at the bench, I remembered Dale eating me as dessert, and I was gone. The dream swept me from reality into a writhing, panting, mess on the floor. At least that's how I was when I came back to the here and now.

"Goddess, no more thinking about the first time a guy stuck his face down there." Which, of course, didn't help as I swept into the memory of how good Dale was with his lips and tongue. Thankfully, I'd set the timer, and the loud noise brought me startling back to reality.

Struggling to move my quaking body, I killed the noise. Checking on dinner, I turned the temperatures down to warm only before I went to the bathroom to freshen up. That included a fresh set of knickers.

When I came out, I opened all the windows and doors in the apartment. Turning on the exhaust fan, I spritzed air freshener everywhere to try and mask my pheromones. When Dale finally walked in, my knees started to shake with the effort of holding myself together.

Peering around at all the open windows and doors, Dale met my eyes and raised a manicured brow over his indigo eyes. Face heating, we both started laughing.

"Thank you for being considerate enough to open the windows, but you don't need to freeze to death."

That's when I noticed I was shivering. Was that because I was cold? I didn't feel cold. Following Dale's eyes to my chest, I crossed my arms to hide how hard my nipples were. It looked like I was smuggling smarties in my bra. Maybe I was cold, or just really, really...

"Vera!" Dale sighed. "Dinner smells wonderful."

Taking the hint, I moved to the kitchen to get plates ready. "How was your day?"

Dale grimaced. "Hard. Quite literally, hard. I'm bonded to a randy female who can't stop thinking about my head between her thighs."

My eyes went to his crotch, and as I did, he grew hard again. Gripping the counter to prevent another daydream, I swallowed a mouthful of desire. "This isn't going to ease is it?"

"It's going to get worse, Vera." Removing his jacket, Dale then toed off his shoes and socks. "At this rate, you are going to spend the night in fevered dreams, possibly tomorrow as well."

Staring helplessly as Dale unbuttoned his shirt, I bit my lip. As Dale stepped towards me, my body temperature rose. Sweat beaded on my skin, and moisture pooled between my thighs. When his hands unzipped his pants and pushed them down his hips, I licked my lips and took a shaking step towards him.

"I'm scared," I whispered as I lowered the zip on my dress.

Pupils dilating as I dropped the dress to the ground, Dale inhaled. "I know."

"You promise you won't hurt me?"

"Only if you ask me for your sexual pleasure."

Reaching behind me, I unclasped my bra, letting it fall. Dale's throat convulsed. I couldn't meet his eyes; they were too intense. Hot everywhere, I trembled where I stood. With a deep breath, I hooked my thumbs inside the band of my knickers and slid them down my thighs. "I still want a wedding."

Striding towards me, Dale nodded. "It's already arranged for tomorrow evening." With a sweep of his arm, Dale cuffed my neck and pulled me towards him.

Our lips crashed together, grunts escaping our throats as our bodies collided. Dale's body was so hard and firm. His strength felt in the muscles bunching under his skin. The firm grasp of Dale's fingers, the eager pinch of his lips, transmitted Dale's impatience.

Dropping to my knees, I longed to taste him. Fisting my hair, Dale waited for me to take him as far as I could into my mouth, then he trembled. "Goddess, Vera!" Pulling himself free, Dale fell on me as he pushed me to the ground under him. "I can't wait any longer. You deserve more, but I can't, not this time."

Shifting between my thighs, Dale found my moist opening with his leaking tip. "I promise I'll make this up to you." Crushing my mouth in a kiss, Dale shoved into me.

My nails scratching his back, I cried out. Malcolm didn't believe in foreplay, but I wasn't quite ready for Dale, despite the day of wet dreams. Dale had a little more girth than I was used to, and my body's initial response was, *'what the ...?'*

Holding my hip with one hand, Dale forced his way inside, burying as deep as he could get. Squirming his hips, Dale adjusted his position and settled his weight on his hands. Once he'd found his leverage, Dale pounded my body. It hurt, a little. More so because his body was twice the size of mine as it hammered me into the cold tile floor. But that was nothing to the absolute relief.

Wrapping my thighs around his waist, I scratched his torso and arms and cried out his name over and over until I came. Roaring his victory, Dale thrust even harder. Veins straining in his neck, Dale released his bottled-up desire, filling me, and then some.

When Dale went to roll away, I went with him, keeping him inside me as I moved to straddle him. "I'm not finished."

Pressing my hands to his chest, I rocked over his hardness. His fluid seeped from between us, the head of his cock flicked back and forth across my cervix. The pressure built again.

Staring into his lust-filled eyes, I placed Dale's hand to my breast and encouraged him to squeeze. Dale complied, a wicked grin trying to emerge across his satisfied face. My body seized, and I came again, milking him. My entire body trembling as I fell forward and let my forehead rest on his chest.

Molasses seeped through my body. It felt like Dale injected me with some sort of hot syrup, and it was creeping through my blood-stream. It felt good, right, and I knew without asking that it was the bond, joining us together for the rest of our lives.

When I thought about what that meant, I started trembling. Without warning, tears fell from my eyes, and I cried. Encircling me in his arms, Dale held me tight. "Shh, I know you weren't ready. I'm sorry, Vera. I promise I'm still going to marry you, and tomorrow night, I'll make love to you."

"Promise you'll come for me?"

"I thought I just did," Dale teased.

Lifting my tear-stained face to view his, I shook my head. "When he finds me, he'll take me. My last term, you have to come for me. Don't let him have me again, but you're not allowed to get hurt either. I couldn't stand to see you hurt, so you can't get hurt."

Dale's smile vanished. His thumb caressed in front of my ear, the rest of his fingers threading into my messed hair. "I'm to play the knight in shining armor and not get my armor dirty?"

"Yes."

Searching my eyes, Dale swallowed as the indigo shifted in his. "Vera, I'm about to let my wolf free. I don't want you to freak out or scream. He won't hurt you, understood?"

Rolling us, Dale set himself on top of me again. His body changing, swelling larger, black fur covering him, but he was still in man form.

My heart was thumping in my chest as I watched Dale turn into a beast. "Dale?"

"Don't scream."

As I watched, Dale's jaw cracked and his face reformed into a wolf-man hybrid. When Dale roared, I caught sight of his incisors, which appeared fantastically dangerous.

My stomach hollowed, I panicked feeling tingling through my body. "Dale?"

My hand cramped. Stretching out my fingers, I tried to relieve the pain. Awed, I watched my fingers elongate, claws protruding from the tips. My eyes widened as the other hand followed.

My skin tingled like popping candy on the tongue. Gasping, my back bowed, and a wave of nausea swept over me, washing the tingling away. When I could look at myself, strawberry-cream colored fur covered my body. Only my nipples remained exposed.

Dale's brown-amber wolf eyes smiled down at me, the indigo edge the only way I could tell that it was still Dale above me. Pulling away from me, Dale observed my hybrid body with appreciation.

My eyes went straight to his humongous penis, pointing right out at me. It wasn't just Dale's muscles that grew in his hybrid form. Dale and Alpha combined in an intoxicating mix - pure power moved before me. Power so strong that no one, woman or wolf could resist his will. Grasping my hip, he rolled me over. My vision swam and changed as he did. A terrible pressure crushed my jaw, and I cried out in pain.

'Let it happen. You're undergoing your first change. You're safe, nothing will hurt you.'

Instinct told me to believe the guttural version of Dale in my head. Closing my eyes, I stretched my jaw. The pressure relieved with cracking inside my head and tingling in my teeth. As long as I kept trying to open my jaw, it didn't hurt.

Pressing a knee between my thighs, Alpha spread them as he pulled my hips up a little. Trying to lift to all fours for him, I stopped when a clawed hand pressed down on my shoulder.

Terrified and enthralled, I whimpered. My emotions contradicted each other, leaving me feeling unsure. Nipping the back of my neck, Alpha soothed me as he settled his body above mine, seeking my opening. Desire pulsed through me, and I turned my bum up a little more, offering myself to him. In my womb, I felt needy and itchy. My Alpha's pleasure was going to soothe that too. Gripping the ground beneath me, I whimpered in need.

When Alpha nipped my neck again, I felt like a cat in catnip. His scent was forest pine and happy with my response, and that delighted me. Behind me, there was a gruff laugh. Goddess, I felt like a puppy playing in the grass for the first time. Every scent was exciting, every touch and sensation.

As Alpha pressed into me, two things came to mind. I was the happiest puppy in the world with the vocal appreciation coming from my Alpha. I was also an exceptionally randy female, craving my mate to fuck me until I howled.

Alpha didn't disappoint. His howl bounced off the walls of the apartment, while my vision exploded in muted colors. My breathing ragged, my jaw moving, but unable to voice how amazing it felt to please your mate like that.

While I was aware of the human comparison, I couldn't describe them. The sensations were entirely different. In this form, the pleasure derived was from his desire. Alpha wanted me for months, so I was floating on cloud nine with all his happy, satisfied, hormones.

With a final nip on my neck, I felt the pressure of his will forcing me to yield. Pressing my forehead to the tiles, I whimpered. A moment later, my entire body shivered. Cracking resounded in my head, cramping in my jaw, hands, and feet, making me stretch to try and relieve it.

Falling limp and human again to the tiled floors, I panted dripping sweat. "Dale?"

Rubbing my back, Dale pressed against my side so I could feel him. "I'm right here. You handled that well."

"Did you know that was going to happen?" Still stretching and flexing my human fingers, I felt rung out and exhausted.

Placing a kiss on my shoulder, Dale sighed. His saliva stung a little, and I squirmed under his lips. "I suspected. My wolf knew. It's why it insisted on taking you that way."

Reaching over my shoulder, I touched the tender flesh, but Dale brushed my fingers away. "I bit you when you submitted to me. It will heal, but it needs a few minutes."

Slumping back onto the cold tiles, I closed my eyes. "Why did you suspect?"

Dale started drawing lazily through the sweat on my back. "Your eyes shifted at the photoshoot. You got excited about a wolf mating with a human woman, but when I looked at your eyes, they were amber. I suspected, if I let Alpha have you, he would use his will over you and bring you into your wolf."

"Because he's stronger than me?"

Dale chuckled like I'd said something humorous. "My wolf has never desired someone before, Viridia, and he desired you before I even realized you were my mate."

Rolling away, I sat up staring at Dale. "What did you call me?"

"My wolf knows your true name now, I like it, I..."

"Don't! Neither of you. Don't call me that. That's the name he uses. It's how I know the difference, so don't use it."

Ignoring how Dale was gawking at me, I got to my feet and ran into the bedroom, but not to cry. I wanted to tear something apart. I ached to rip Malcolm apart. He'd stolen fourteen years of happiness from me. I hated him even more for having taken my time with Dale. Growling in frustration, I stormed into the bathroom. I was sticky and sweaty, and messy, and I needed a shower.

Standing under the water, I was rinsing the soap away when Dale's body pressed against the back of mine. His lips kissed that spot on my shoulder, but it didn't hurt so much now.

"I'm one of the strongest alphas in our country. You were always going to submit to me, mate, or no mate. The difference between Malcolm and I? I wouldn't have needed violence to get you to lift your tail to me. An alpha male like me-"

"Females just go weak at the knees." I understood why, plus I'd seen even the human women swoon in his presence.

"My own daughters would submit to me if I were so inclined. I'm not." Dale kissed my shoulder, hesitating over his next words. "You're a strong female, that's why he had to force you. His will couldn't control you."

"Did you just admit you can control me?"

Dale shifted, that alone was his answer. "If I were the sort of man to do that, you'd have invited me to your bed the night I invited you to dinner at the house. I would only ever use my will on you to keep you safe, Vera, or, to help you shift back into your human form, as I did now."

"I didn't shift completely?"

Rubbing my upper arms, Dale nuzzled my neck. "I held you in beast form. A full shift can be painful for the first few times. For what Alpha wanted, the beast form was less painful but achieved the same outcome. If you so choose, Wednesday night, I can help you take your wolf form."

Excited and terrified, I turned to face him. Caressing my cheek,

Dale placed a gentle kiss to my mouth. Desire ran hot through my body, making me gasp. "Dale, can you fuck me again?"

My chest filled with radiant joy when Dale smiled. Crushing his mouth to mine, Dale lifted my thighs to his waist.

By the time we left the shower and actually sat down for dinner, it was quite dry but still edible. "Can I make a suggestion? From now on, allow enough time for a romp before dinner. If I've been away from you all day, I'm going to want a serving of you before I eat."

"How long would you suggest?" Batting my eyes at him.

Rising from his chair, Dale stalked towards me. "A good half an hour should suffice for the first course."

Without another word, Dale swept the tabletop of its dishes. Everything cluttered to the floor as he pulled me out of the chair and pushed me over the table.

"Dale we've just eaten."

Lifting my skirt, Dale smacked my bum playfully before pulling my scanties down. "There is still the lounge and bed to defile, Vera, so don't expect much sleep tonight."

As his finger tested my readiness, I moaned. "We have tomorrow night."

"Oh, I'm taking you to a fancy hotel for our wedding night, Sweet Pea. It should be special, after all. Now, what was that fantasy you had in the board room?"

CHAPTER 21

"*I* do."

The smile on my face only outdone by the one on Dale's as I promised myself to him. Tears glistened in my eyes. My cup overflowed with joy.

"I now pronounce you man and wife. You can kiss your bride."

Applause broke out around us. Dale's eyes sparkling as he pulled me into him and bent me over backward with the force of his kiss.

We were in the park opposite Dale's apartment. Somehow he'd managed to organize a celebrant, licenses, and someone to decorate overnight. Jeremy and Bob stood as groomsmen. Alexa and Hymn were my bridesmaids - something they'd sprung on me at the park. A few other members of the pack, like Adam and Jonathan, attended, but the honor fell to Cameron, Dale's son, to give me away.

Some of their work colleagues from Dale's agency came, which is what drew the crowd of passersby's. Considering well-dressed models were guests, the public thought we were celebrities or something. So, the immense applause was from a bunch of strangers who didn't even know us.

A limo transported us to the yacht club, where an impromptu

reception was ready for twenty guests. We ate and drank, posed for photos, and even cut the traditional wedding cake.

As I appraised the beautiful decorations, I shook my head in awe and gazed up at my husband. "How did you pull all this together?"

"Alexa and Hymn. They've been to a ton of weddings and always wanted to be bridesmaids. So, they were over the moon to put this together for you."

Turning to find the twins, I thanked them for making it even more amazing then I imagined. Hymn shrugged. "You grew up human, it's natural you would have wanted the big human shindig."

Alexa laughed. "Come off it, Hymn. If you ever met your mate, you'd want the big white wedding too."

Hymn tried to dismiss it as unimportant, but the flicker in her eye told me Alexa was right. "Anyway, you still need to throw the bouquet," Hymn demanded, handing me my flowers.

The girls gathered all the single females for the bouquet toss. Hymn barreled everyone over to catch it.

"Told you she wanted to get married." Rubbing her jaw where Hymn's flying elbow connected, Alexa grimaced.

Taking my hand, Dale spun me under his arm. "Come dance with me." Moving us to an open space, Dale pulled me in against him and started swaying us. "Are you happy, Vera?"

Meeting his eyes, I expect the happiness in mine reflected the pure joy in his. "It's more than I ever dreamed of, thank you."

"I want to give you everything, Vera. Everything your heart desires, I want you to have."

My heart exploded. "I've always wanted to see snow, and have a snowball fight. I've wanted to swim under a waterfall. Go hang gliding. See a live opera and ballet. Go on a picnic in the park, play on swings. Oh, visit a fair and ride the dodgem cars - I don't know what they are, but I've heard it's so much fun…"

Listening to me, Dale smiled. His eyes shining while I rattled off all the things I'd ever wanted to do that I could remember on the spot. He waited until I took a breath and seemed to finish. "Is that all?"

It was sarcasm, I was sure. I doubt Dale would remember them.

But the last two, the things that I wanted more than anything, these I hoped he could give me.

"I want to go to university and study. I want a proper degree and qualification. And..." This last thing I desired, and yet, I feared it was the one thing no one could give me.

"And?" Dale pressed, lifting my chin so I would meet his eyes. His smile faded as he saw the tears threatening to spill from mine.

"I want a baby. I want to be a mum."

Lips twitching, Dale pulled me closer and put his mouth to my ear. "It may not be straight away, but I believe I can fulfill all your desires."

"Really? You're not just saying that?"

"Vera, I intend to breed with you." That cheeky grin I adored spread across his handsome face. "I'm certainly going to enjoy practicing at every opportunity. Speaking of which, it's time I took you away and consummated our vows." Holding my hand, Dale led me over to Jeremy where he whispered in his ear.

Lips quirking, Jeremy got everyone's attention. "It's time for the bride and groom to leave!"

"Keen much?" Bob called out, everyone laughed.

"You are all invited to keep celebrating, but let's give our best wishes to the bride and groom." Eyes twinkling, Jeremy was the first to claim hugs from us.

Everyone cheered and clapped as Dale led me out, stopping for everyone to hug and congratulate us on the way out.

The limousine was waiting, and once Dale had me in the back seat, he pulled me onto his lap and kissed me.

"How far away is the hotel?" I breathed against his mouth when his hands found me beneath the dress.

"Ten minutes." Pulling the gusset of my scanties aside, Dale spread my lips with the smooth head of him. "Long enough for the first course."

Pressing my hips down, I bit my lip, moaning at the pure relief of having him inside me again. Within a matter of minutes, I was cumming, my body coercing Dale to join it in wedded bliss.

By the time the valet opened the door at the hotel, we were sitting in our seats, my face flushed and hair a little messed.

Taking me to the suite, Dale turned on the taps to fill the couple's bath. Smiling as he watched me try and find the zip, Dale pulled me closer to him and eased it down.

While undressing, Dale kissed and touched me until we both stood naked. When the bath was ready, Dale stepped into it, holding my hand to help me in and pulled me against him.

Taking his time, Dale washed my body. Running his hands over my wet skin, he took the time to learn the contours of my physique. When he finished, I turned and concentrated on his body. Kissing languidly while my hands memorized him. When I shifted my body over his and took him inside me, Dale purred. It made me laugh. "I didn't know wolves purred?"

"Only when they are inside you, Vera."

Our body's swaying together, we kissed and caressed each other. As we started making waves in the tub, Dale lifted me, standing with my legs still around his waist as he stepped out. Snatching a towel from the rail, Dale carried me into the bedroom, lying me out on the toweling and kneeling on the floor.

"Did I mention I love how you taste?" Dale rumbled as he tugged my hips closer to him. With a swipe of his tongue, he stole my breath. Dale then to lick and suck me until I was thrashing around on the bed, pulling his hair and crying out his name.

As I fell back to earth, Dale stood and knelt between my shaking thighs. A smile covered his face, and his eyes shining in the dim lighting, making them almost blue. As he lowered his body over mine, I couldn't help but mimic his smile.

"What?" Dale dropped a kiss on my chin before his mouth found the twin peaks of my breasts.

"I'm so glad I'm your wife. Beyond happy that I said yes to letting you bite me. Relieved that I purchased that house and let alpha sniff me."

Lifting his face to mine, Dale hovered over my lips, brushing my mouth. "Me too."

THE SUN WAS STREAMING in the window when I woke. Moaning at the slight ache in my body from the second night of fantastic sex, I opened my eyes and found the bed empty.

"Dale?" Sitting up, I glanced around the suite. There was no response. Frowning, I grabbed the towel that Dale discarded on the floor between round two and three. Or, when Dale became beast and brought me into mine again.

Dale's surprise when I'd grown a tail this time made me smile. I'd pushed him off me to strut around the room swishing it too and fro, hugging it and stroking it. Allowing my fascination, Dale told me he wanted me. Feeling cheeky, I batted my eyelashes while circling him. Strutting with my tail, I accused him of being jealous because he didn't have such a lovely tail.

Before my next tail swish, Dale pinned me face-first against the bedroom wall. Biting my shoulder until I whimpered, Dale told me to lift that lovely tail for him. I'd loved every minute of the past twenty-four hours.

"Dale?"

Searching the suite, I found a tray filled with breakfast, still covered and warm with a note in the lounge room.

YOU LOOKED BEAUTIFUL ASLEEP, *I couldn't bear to wake you. Come to work when you are ready. Jeremy can fill in for you until you arrive, and then he will take you home afterward.*

If I don't see you at work, I'll see you tonight.

Your loving husband and mate.

TODAY WAS my first day as the photographer for the underground media shoot. Shoving a piece of toast between my teeth, I ran into the bedroom and pulled out the clothes I needed.

Noticing Dale's bag was gone already, I showered and ate while dressing. Grabbing up my luggage, I dropped the room keys into the quick checkout box. Forty minutes later, I was exiting the elevator onto Dale's office floor.

"Good morning, Mrs. Hearn." Caprice was at the wedding last night.

"I'm late, I know, can you tell me where to find Jeremy?"

Clucking her tongue, Caprice smiled. "You should be on your honeymoon, not working. Everyone can forgive a new bride for being late the day after her wedding. Jeremy is in the closed studio for private shoots. It's two floors down and to the right when you come out of the elevator. There will be a sign on the door."

"Thanks, Caprice." Pressing the elevator button, I gnawed my lip. What on earth made me think I could handle a real job in a company?

"Mrs. Hearn, would you like me to put your bag in your husband's office?" Coming to my side, Caprice held out her hand for my overnight case.

Passing her the handle, I sighed in relief that she was so lovely. "Thanks, Caprice."

Two floors down, I found the door marked 'closed shoot' and knocked. No one answered, so I opened the door and let myself in before closing it again. The room was dark, but there was some light coming from further into the room. Loud music was playing further back in the studio, drowning out all other sounds. Considering the shoot yesterday, there was more than likely a reason for that.

"Jeremy?"

"He's on the other side of the screen." Appearing out of the darkness next to me, Howard was shirtless; a pair of jeans riding low. If I didn't already dislike him, I'd have appreciated the view of his v pack. But the personality in his eyes made it worth nothing.

"You're okay near me now, right?"

Howard's eyes grew angry. "I'm never going to be alright around a bitch like you."

Sucking in a breath, I backed up into the door as he stepped closer, getting in my face.

"I know what you did to your last alpha. Bitches like you are only good for one thing." Setting an arm each side of my shoulders, Howard trapped me. "I get you alone, I'm going to show you exactly what that is. Then, I'm going to break that pretty neck of yours, so you don't destroy this pack like you did your own."

Tears running down my cheeks, I met his dark eyes.

"You tell my alpha, and I'll tell him you're making it up to get rid of me, that you are trying to poison our pack like you did yours. Who do you think he's going to believe? His pack mate he's known decades, or the piece of ass he's spent a night getting his balls off in?"

Hating the proximity of this man, I recoiled from his onion breath suffocating my space. I wanted to stand firm, but the doubt still lingered, choking me with fear and uncertainty. "I'm his mate."

"You must be stupid to believe that cock and bull. Dale told you that to get in your pants. You think that the wedding was real yesterday?" Dropping one hand, he groped my breast intending to cause pain. "You can be my mate too if that makes you feel better?"

Knocking his hand away, I shoved him back from me, but he didn't budge.

"When Dale's finished with you, Jeremy will be your mate for a while too. Then Bob. We can pass you around, and all have a go being your mate."

When Howard tried to touch me again, I knocked his hand away, getting angrier by the minute.

"Hell, if you're a good fuck, we'll keep you around like a party favorite."

My eyes itched, jaw throbbing too. My fingers were cramping as I stepped into Howard. Doing as Jeremy taught me, I swiped my fingernails across his abdomen to back him away from me. Smile dropping, Howard stumbled back, confusion clouding his face.

"You'll never touch me. If you try, I'll rip your throat out."

The lights came on as Jeremy strode toward us, his eyes hard and suspicious. "What's going on here? I told you to bring Vera to me."

Bottom lip trembling, Howard choked, his eyes wide. "The bitch can shift."

Glancing at me, Jeremy shoved Howard's shoulder, forcing him further away from me. "Are you high? She's standing there entirely human."

That's when Howard stared at something, his face pale. Jeremy and I followed his gaze and saw the blood. Five large gouges across his abdomen, and a hell of a lot of blood.

CHAPTER 22

*Y*ears ago, I read a scene in a book about a detective puking all over the mutilated body, destroying evidence. At the time, I thought, *'as if that would happen?'* You'd turn your head and vomit elsewhere. Now, I understood. As soon as I saw the bloody gashes in Howard's abdomen, I threw up all over his feet and the pool of blood beneath him.

"Shit, Vera!" Grabbing my shoulders, Jeremy moved me away from Howard, across the room to an open window. "Stay here and breathe."

Slumping against the open window, I sucked the fresh air in, still horrified by what happened.

"You're concerned about her when I'm the one bleeding?!"

"Did you want her vomiting in your wounds?"

"What's going on?" Hymn appeared in a slinky dress from the set. "What the hell?"

"Shift and heal," Jeremy ordered.

"Fuck that, let our alpha see what his bitch is capable of doing."

Shaking her head at Howard, Hymn started back to the set. "I'll call him, but you want to have a good reason for refusing a direct order from your beta."

"You're pathetic," Jeremy growled, walking away from Howard.

"You're all blind not to see she's a problem. Just because she's full-blood doesn't make her a nice person. She destroyed her last pack, and she'll destroy ours too."

Gripping his hair in his fist, Jeremy scowled. "How?"

Watching Jeremy, I suspected this wasn't the first time he heard this rant. "She's mated. Her pheromones only call to her mate. My instinct is no longer to mate with her, but to protect her."

"Mine haven't changed."

Jeremy glared at his cousin. "Which makes me wonder about your loyalty."

Mouth falling open, Howard paled. "What do you mean?"

"You still desire our Alpha's mate; that's not her pheromones but your jealousy. You disobeyed a direct order from me, twice, today. The only way that could happen is if you have betrayed your pack, and your connection to us is waning."

A gasp behind us alerted us to Hymn's return. "Oh, Goddess! What did you do?"

Eyes flicking to me, thoughts flashed across Howard's face like a neon screen.

The impact was a sledgehammer to my chest. "You told Malcolm I was alive."

A growl near the door warned us that Dale had walked in unnoticed and heard enough. Stealing the oxygen from our lungs, Dale's rage blew through the room like a firestorm.

Sinking to the floor, I hid behind my knees, trembling as I watched my very pissed off alpha breeze into the room. Jeremy and Hymn were backing up, Jeremy placing himself in front of Hymn and me.

Grabbing Howard by the throat, Dale lifted him into the air. "Why?"

"She was driving us crazy and driving us away from our home. I was waking up outside her house, trying to find a way into her. I was going crazy, needing to take her, but your orders refused to let me. She was a constant ache, and it was killing me. She was killing me, killing our pack. She had to go."

Dropping Howard, Dale snarled in disgust. "What did you tell

161

him?" There was an undercurrent in Dale's voice which threatened violence. I hid my head between my knees like I was on a plane about to crash.

"That his bitch was still alive and making herself comfortable with a new alpha."

My head snapped up, teeth and jaw itching to run over there and rip his throat out. Dale's will brushed over me, placating me with his pride of my eagerness, but ordering me to stay.

"Idiot!" Jeremy seethed. Despite his outward calm appearance, we could all feel Dale's rage.

Goddess, Dale looked so sexy in that suit, all that power and strength radiating off him. Tempting me to crawl to him and wrap myself around his muscular thigh, and breathe his scent into me.

Dale's golden eyes turned towards me. "Not now, Sweet Pea."

Pouting, I saw Dale's lips twitch like he was trying not to laugh. His anger hesitated as if distracted. Glancing at me, Dale raised a brow.

"Oh, sorry." Placing my forehead on my knees, I tried to keep my mind on Howard's betrayal. "Perhaps, I should leave?"

"Good idea," Hymn murmured holding out her hand. "Let the men deal with this, us bitches," she snarled the word in Howard's direction, "will go get a coffee."

Looking to Dale for permission, I didn't dare move until he gave me a slight nod.

Howard launched to his feet. "No, you can't let her leave, she attacked me. She can shift."

Blinking, Howard was back on the floor several meters away. Groaning, and blood spurting from his nose. As Dale's anger fire balled through the room, I whimpered.

"Leave!"

Hymn snatched my hand, and we ran out the door. We didn't stop running until we were three flights down on the fire stairs. That's when Hymn turned to me. "You can shift?"

"Only when your father wills me too."

"Obviously not, if you partial shifted in there when you got angry. Could dad make me shift to full-wolf?"

"I haven't done that yet. We're trying that tonight." Glancing up the stairs, I bit my lip. "Or we were."

"Why does that scare you?"

"Howard said some things-"

"Howard was raving like a madman in there. Don't worry about it."

"He wasn't raving before Jeremy interrupted. Actually, he was very sane and clear in his thoughts. Just like he would have needed to be when he called Malcolm to tell him I'm still alive. It's not like he had his number to drunk dial him, is it?"

Throat contracting, Hymn inhaled audibly. "No. Only the Alpha's on the Liderii have each Alpha's number. For Howard to get it, he would have had to break into Dale's office, seek out the information, and use it."

"He also would have been sane on the phone. If he were raving like he was up there, Malcolm would have dismissed it as a prank."

"That unsettles you? Howard has his issues, but he's not totally insane."

"I'd rather prefer he was."

Crossing her arms, Hymn stood insulted for her packmate. "What's that supposed to mean?"

"It means, I don't think Howard is insane at all. He wasn't going crazy with my pheromones if it didn't affect the others that way. It means I don't believe a word Howard said while he was raving up there. That was an act because he got caught. Howard didn't like Dale finding his mate, and he's determined to get rid of me for some reason."

Blinking at me, Hymn bit her lip and glanced back up the stairs.

"Hymn?" Stepping closer to her, I knew I'd hit on something. "What aren't you telling me?"

"You may have realized Dale's the only one with children in the pack? Only the alpha breeds in a pack. If another does, they either leave and start their own pack, or if the current Alpha isn't breeding, he steps aside."

"Dale was stepping aside for Howard?"

"No. But he's Liderii now, has been for many years, and he's been Alpha since we were born. Dad announced, if someone else were to breed, he would step aside."

"Why wouldn't they breed anyway?"

"Only the strong males, the ones strong enough to be Alpha are fertile. People often confuse Alpha for meaning they are the strongest. But it's actually about virility. It so happens that being the strongest and most virile male in the pack attracts females. Which is usually why the Alpha gets to be a breeder."

"So, all your males have been out there sowing their wild oats in the hope of becoming the next Alpha, then I come along. But I'm a purebred; it's renowned we are infertile? So why does it matter?"

Hymn bit her lip as she thought about her words. "The male granted the blessing of a full-blood female as a mate is a Goddess declared Alpha. He would automatically become Alpha of a pack. Since Dale is already Alpha, it means he's Alpha for life. Anyone wanting to breed now would need to leave and start their own pack."

"That's an issue?"

"We're a family, Vera. I know the concept is foreign to you, but we love and care for each other. We protect each other. We'd be giving that up."

Licking my lips, hurt by her belief that I didn't know what a family was, I kept my mind on gaining information. "Not even for the chance to have your own children?"

"Not for me, no." Turning on her heel, Hymn entered the corridor. Following her to the elevator, we waited. When the lift arrived, we stepped in, and Hymn pressed the ground floor button.

Hymn side-glanced me. "I don't want you to get the wrong idea. The majority of the pack are happy for you. Both, that you found each other, and that you escaped what was happening to you."

"Some just would have preferred I not be a full-blood?"

"They envy him. He's virile, strong, and the Goddess has shown him favoritism. But there is a difference between envy and jealousy.

Envy is a longing for someone else's good fortunes. Jealousy is far more nefarious."

"Howard is jealous."

Hymn nodded. "That was the case long before you arrived, but you became the jewel in our Alpha's crown. Dad's been a great alpha, I'm happy for him to stay my Alpha until he dies. Howard was angry when Jeremy got made beta over him, and then Bob delta. That's when he started on the drugs all those years ago. He's never felt good enough."

"That's because he isn't."

Turning to face me, Hymn gawped at me. "Wow, that was bitchy."

"It's the truth."

"Yeah, I know. I just didn't expect you to say it out loud." Hymn smirked. "Get a girl laid and look what happens."

Cheeks hot, I averted my gaze as the elevator doors slid open.

Hymn laughed as we exited into the lobby. "I need some serious coffee. This morning has been way too intense."

Directing me to her favorite coffee shop, I couldn't agree with her more. Now, I had a better understanding of why Howard didn't like me, and the political underpinnings of a pack. I also knew how Malcolm discovered I lived and was somewhat relieved it wasn't a mistake I made by leaving a trail. But that wouldn't save me now.

"If something happens to me, Dale loses his crown, doesn't he?"

Staring into her coffee, Hymn mourned. "Vera, you are bound. If you die, so would my dad."

My throat constricted with the idea that Dale's fate rested with mine. "Howard said the mate thing was a lie to get in my pants." I almost wanted his lie to be true now. It wasn't; I could feel Dale's moods like they were my own and hear his thoughts. Though, not as well as he could mine, it seemed.

"You know Howard was goading you."

"Hymn, am I selfish? It's just, Dale seems to be able to sense my moods and hear my thoughts, but I rarely feel his."

Blowing out a breath, Hymn leaned back in her chair. "Selfish would be a harsh way of describing you. You've spent your life keenly aware of the moods of others and hiding away from them. I would say that you close yourself off; that you're insulated. You feel your mate, but you don't acknowledge you do because it scares you. You more than likely feel his mood, but don't realize it's his."

"Jeremy has me keeping a diary of my moods. He wanted me to note when they changed."

"Sounds like something Jeremy would do. He studied psychology decades ago. He's probably working a way to get you to acknowledge the bond." Hymn smirked at me. "What are you feeling now?"

"Calm with an undercurrent of homicidal tendencies. I also want to pack my bags and high tail it out of here before Malcolm finds me."

Hymn nodded. "I'd say those first two are your Alpha because we are all feeling his rage right now. The fear, that's all yours."

"It always has been."

CHAPTER 23

"*V*era." Jeremy marched into Dale's office, placing a folder on his desk. "I'll take you home."

"Dale?"

"He's angry and still has to finish his workday. Best to wait for him to cool down." Hoisting my bag, Jeremy held the door for me.

Following obediently, I kept a bit of distance between Jeremy and me. As a member of the pack, Jeremy held rank over me as the beta. His job was to protect me, and that meant I do as told when he gave an order.

No one had to tell me this, it was something I felt in my bones. Bob and Jeremy were the only two, other than Dale, who could give me an order and expect me to follow it. Bob's, I felt I might be able to challenge; Jeremy, not a chance.

The drive home was quiet with Jeremy withdrawn and angry. Getting in an enclosed space with him took more energy than I had left today. So I was huddling against the door and focused on the passing scenery.

As we pulled into the driveway, Jeremy sighed. "I still need to do the shopping. I'll drop you off and head back out. Is there anything different you need?"

Doing a quiet inventory of my fridge in my mind, I shook my head. "I was cooking dinner for Dale tonight."

"He'll be here at the normal time. With my mood, its best if we skip on the self-defense lessons today."

"I understand."

Parking the car, Jeremy carried my bag to the front door for me. "Will you be okay?"

"This is the only place I've ever felt safe."

"That will need to change, Vera. You are mated now; you should be living in the main house with your mate."

"Not today, Jeremy."

Nodding, Jeremy waited for me to unlock the door. "I'll bring your shopping down later."

"Thanks." Stepping inside, I closed and locked the door as usual. Feeling a little insecure, I made my way through the house, checking all the windows and doors first.

Hanging the wedding dress in my room so I could sit on my bed and gaze at it, I smiled at the memories that dress brought me. With a sigh, I went out and made myself some lunch, deciding what to cook for dinner while I was there. Sitting down at my computer, I did some work but found I wasn't much in the mood for it.

The knock at the door actually excited me. For once, I was happy for Jeremy to be dropping off my shopping. "Bob?"

"Jeremy asked me to bring your shopping down. He's packing up Howard's things."

Stepping aside to let Bob in, I shut the door after him and followed him to the kitchen.

Placing the bags on the kitchen bench, Bob grinned. "So, how was the wedding night?" Heat filled my face remembering. "That good?" When I grew hotter around the collar, Bob started laughing. "From what I hear, Dale was smiling pretty big the morning of the wedding. Jeremy also tells me you were causing orgies the day before that."

"How much do I owe?"

"You're pack now, Vera, Dale gets your bills." Heading back to the door, Bob winked. "Try not to trash the kitchen tonight."

Imagining doing that, I smiled at the possibility. Bob laughed as he shut the door after himself, locking it for me.

Deciding I wanted to be fresh when Dale arrived, I went and had a shower. Planning out dinner as I washed, I decided what I could prepare in advance. It had to be something that wouldn't spoil if Dale and I got caught up for a while after he arrived.

When I finished the shower, I could hear my phone ringing. Cursing, I wrapped a towel around me and ran out to the bedroom, snatching it up. "Hello?"

"Is everything okay?" Dale asked.

"Yes, why?"

"This is the second time I've rung, and it almost rang out."

"Oh, I was in the shower daydreaming about what to cook you tonight."

"I can't make it." My stomach sank. "I fired Howard today and told him to leave the pack. Before he left, he deleted an entire month's worth of work. I'm dealing with our customers while IT try and recover it."

"Oh!" I bit my lip. "He's not coming here is he?"

"No. I've barred him from the property and told Jeremy to deliver his stuff to him. He's meeting him at his city apartment in an hour. I can't believe he betrayed me like that."

"I'm sorry."

"It started before you came along, Vera. Don't take this on yourself."

For a minute, we both fell quiet. "So you're not coming home tonight?"

"No, I'm sorry. Had I known earlier, I would have kept you in the city with me."

"It's okay. I like it here."

"I know, but I'm uneasy about you being so far away from me." Dale took a deep breath. "Vera, I want you to go stay in the main house for the rest of the week. You can cook for everyone up there."

"I'm not ready."

"Vera, please?"

Sighing at the plea in his voice, I huffed. "I'll go up later."

"Before sunset."

"Okay," I agreed to make him happy.

"I'll call you before bed tonight. I love you."

Unsure how to answer his farewell, I hung up and put the phone on the bedside table. Was I ready to go stay in the packhouse? I wasn't sure, but I'd promised Dale I would, so I turned to go repack my bag.

A man was standing in my bedroom door, bringing me to an abrupt halt. "Please be a dream?" My breath hitched, and tears started falling immediately because I knew it wasn't. He was standing there watching me.

"Viridia." Stepping into my room, Malcolm yanked his belt out of the belt loops and doubled it over in his hand. "I've never seen your skin so unblemished. You've always been beautiful, but without the bruises, you are stunning."

When Malcolm touched my cheek, I winced away but froze at the look in his eyes. Waiting for a second, Malcolm placed his palm to the side of my face.

Grimacing at his contact, I turned my face away. "I found my mate. You can't take me back."

Malcolm dropped his hand, annoyance singing through the room like a high-pitched chime. "I heard." Malcolm's eyes fell to the towel wrapped around me.

Moving my hand behind my back, I tried to find my phone on the bedside table.

"Don't do that," Malcolm warned in a tone I knew all too well.

Sobbing, I let my hand move away from the side table. When Malcolm moved to untuck the towel, I clenched it tight. "Please, Malcolm, you need to go. You have your pack; I have my mate. I'm where I should have been for the last twelve years. If you abided by tradition, you wouldn't have sent your pack insane."

Malcolm's eyes dilated, causing me to step back from his anger. "I sent them insane? I tried to appease them by letting them have their fun with you. Do you think I wanted to share you? I had no choice because you kept stirring them up. Had you gotten with child like a good woman, I wouldn't have had to fight them off all the time."

"Full-blood women can't bear children. Every Lycan knows that! The tradition to find our mates is there to protect our packs. I've met the Liderii. They told me it was your fault the pack became violent and insane because you didn't follow tradition."

Malcolm stepped back half a step. "Full-blood?"

"Yes. I'm pure Lycan."

"That can't be right."

"I assure you, I'm pure Lycan."

Jaw clenching, Malcolm glared at me, his eyes angrier than they were a moment before. "I didn't know."

"It wouldn't have mattered. What you did to me when I was fourteen showed you didn't care. You conquered my father, and you raped me as another way to conquer him. You didn't care what or who I was, just that I was the Alpha's daughter."

"Being mated has given you a backbone, Viridia." Grinning maliciously, Malcolm struck his belt across my face with a loud snap.

Falling backward and to the side from the impact, my eyes filled with tears, blinding me. Yanked up, Malcolm threw me on my stomach on the bed. Pinning my hands behind my back, Malcolm strapped them together with his belt.

"I heard you know how to shift to claws now, so let's make sure you can't slash me open again."

"No, Malcolm, please don't do this?"

"Goddess! Can you shut her up? She's so weak and pathetic." My head whipped to the door as Howard walked into my bedroom like he lived here. He hadn't just called Malcolm, he brought him here.

Rolling me onto my back, Malcolm smirked. "I like her pleading; it turns me on."

Snatching the towel, he yanked it off me, throwing it aside. Caressing the scar over my side, Malcolm lowered his fingers to touch the brand he'd given me when I was fourteen.

"See this? This marks you mine, Viridia. I don't care if you met your mate, in fact, that works in my favor because now your pheromones won't send the pack mad."

"She'll be dead after tonight, it won't matter." Tugging his shirt over his head, Howard leaned over my face and spat in my mouth. "I warned you what would happen if I got you alone, Bitch."

Malcolm's eyes burned with fury. "I never agreed to kill her."

"Dale is too strong to take on. If we kill her, it kills him, and I get this pack."

"You're too weak to be Alpha. That's why Jeremy and Bob were higher ranked."

Ear twitching, Malcolm eyed Howard. "You told me you were beta."

Insane bravery taking me over, or it was the knowledge that I would die tonight, I laughed. "He wishes." What was the point in cowering to your death? I didn't want them to rape and torture me first. If I was going to die, I was going to go down swinging.

Growling, Howard smacked me across the face. "Shut up! I'm good enough to be beta."

Despite the sting in my cheek, I kept laughing. After Malcolm's hit, Howard's was a love tap. "I've seen Bob best you. In this room, you're the weak and pathetic one. That's why you hate me. You know you are weaker than me! I survived years of abuse and fought for my freedom. You are a pathetic, jealous asshole who betrayed his own pack. You don't even have loyalty." Taking a breath, I spat in his face, shocking him. "I doubt you could get a woman pregnant. You are probably neutered like a ball-less bull."

"Fucking bitch!" Howard went to hit me.

Blocking his strike, Malcolm threw Howard across the room. "You lied to me. Nothing you told me was the truth. Our deal is off."

Growling, Howard charged Malcolm, shifting as he did. Like liquid flowing over his skin, Malcolm took beast form. Catching Howard around the throat as he came at him, Malcolm threw him across the room. Howard landed with a sickening thud. As Malcolm stomped towards Howard, I got myself upright and to the bedside table. Using my hands to pick up my phone, I ran out of the bedroom.

Pressing the quick-dial for Jeremy, I ran for the back door. Turning to push down on the handle, I whimpered when I found it locked. Shifting my hands to unlock the latch, I dropped the phone. "Jeremy, help!" I yelled when I saw the call connected.

Managing to get the lock open, I was turning the handle when a large hand grabbed my throat. Staring wide-eyed as Malcolm melted back out of beast form to human, I struggled in his hold.

"Where do you think you are going?" Snarling, Malcolm yanked me away from the back door. "You were right about that wolf, Viridia. He was weak, and he was very wrong about you, but that doesn't change a thing. You belong to me."

CHAPTER 24

*F*lying across the room, I hit the wall above the lounge and fell to the sofa with a scream. Pain seared through my body. Fisting my hair, Malcolm pulled me up to standing. Naked after his shift, his excitement was evident.

"You've grown braver in your time away from me, Viridia. You would never have dared speak to any of my wolves like that. I'm impressed."

Fidgeting as he talked, I tried to get out of my restraints. I'd felt the belt loosen when I hit the wall. Fear flooded my system, but instead of it paralyzing me, my brain was racing, thinking of how to get free. Having always been a good runner, I could run. If I could get my hands free, I could run for the main house, and get help. Remembering Jeremy and Dale wasn't there, I sobbed.

Forcing me to my knees, Malcolm pouted. "Come on, Viridia. I was enjoying this new side of you. Don't ruin it with tears."

"Please, Malcolm, don't do this. Let me go. Please?"

Scowling, Malcolm forced me down to lie on the floor and knelt above me. "I can't do that. I love you."

"That's bullshit! You never loved me, never cared for me."

Shaking his head, Malcolm sighed. "You're wrong."

"You don't know what love is. You don't rape a girl because you love her, and you don't beat her out of love. You have spent fourteen years, raping, beating, and humiliating me. That's not love."

"You only remember the bad times. We mostly made love. The beatings only happened when you misbehaved and set the other members of the pack off. I understand now why it got worse over the years, with your pheromones, but it won't be like that anymore. With you mated, we can be together, and love each other without all that hostility."

"I belong to my mate. He loves me and cares for me. Dale has shown me how a real man treats a woman, and the Goddess can damn me before I go back to a life of pain and fear with you."

Malcolm's eyes turned fierce at my comparison with Dale. I swear I lost an entire patch of hair when his fist ripped my head back. My scalp stung, and there was the feel of blood dribbling. "You are mine!"

Hissing in pain, I tried to delay, to hold out long enough for help to arrive. "You're obsessed, and obsession isn't love. If you loved me, you would care how much you are hurting me. Your fixation is about you and how you feel. You are selfish and violent and cruel."

Relaxing his grip, Malcolm snarled at me. "Selfish?"

A strange calm came over me that I'd never experienced. I was goading him, and I wondered if my behavior was suicidal. That subconsciously I decided I'd rather die than go back with him.

"Especially in bed. I've never been able to compare before, but now I know how bad you are at sex."

Rearing back, fist ready and aimed for my head, Malcolm swung. A growl ripped through the night. My back door smashed as something dark-grey came through it and threw Malcolm away from me.

Above me, a massive beast straightened. Covered in dark-grey fur with a white strip down his spine. Goldeyes rimmed in blue checked me over while Malcolm snarled and got to his feet. With a flick of his arms, Malcolm became beast too, but he had nothing on Bob. Bob was over a head taller, and much broader. Bob was stronger.

Malcolm rushed Bob. Swinging his arm, Bob sent Malcolm flying across the room and smashing into my kitchen. Rolling me, Bob slashed his giant claw, sliced the belt restraining me. With my wrists free, he turned his attention to the threatening growl of Malcolm.

Planting his feet, Bob pushed down and pounced. Catching Malcolm, Bob forced him back to the kitchen and away from me. Relief washed over me; Bob was stronger than Malcolm, I could sense it. This should be easy.

But, nothing in my life had ever been easy. As I watched them fight, I learned there was a difference between strength and speed. Malcolm didn't stay Alpha in a hostile pack of madmen because he couldn't fight.

The first time Malcolm got the upper hand on Bob, my heart stopped. As they smashed through the kitchen, my breath stopped, my heart raced, and fear drowned my senses. The fear of someone I cared about getting hurt. Panicking, unable to move, I stared in horror as they fought. The fear paralysis finally kicked in, and I was stuck watching; dreading every hit Bob took to protect me. Fearing for him.

It was all so very new to me. I'd only ever feared other people, never for another. Never had I had to worry about another's safety. Never feared someone dying as a result of trying to help me.

Raking his claws across Bob's chest, Malcolm scored his first real hit. A pressure in my head developed, making me wince. It was like someone yelling in your ears, but it was so loud you actually couldn't hear it. My head hurting under the assault, I didn't know how to relieve the pressure. It didn't matter because, at that moment, Bob stumbled.

Using his speed to grab Bob's throat, Malcolm punched him in the face. Blood spurted from Bob's nose. Without thinking, I caught up a vase and threw it straight at Malcolm's head. As it smashed against the side of his face, he released Bob and turned to me.

Staring down at my hands as Bob renewed his effort, I stood with my mouth hanging open. I'd moved fast. Inhuman-quick. Blood and fur slashed through the air. Following the blur of the beast's battle, I worried I wouldn't see what was happening.

When my eyes itched, I squeezed them shut and rubbed them, taking a second to relieve the itching. When I opened my eyes, the fighting had slowed down, though, it hadn't, I was just able to track it now. The pressure in my head was also gone, the yelling no longer noiseless.

'Run!' Bob yelled at me. 'Vera, run.'

Bob hit the window. It wobbled like jelly from his impact. Rebounding off, Bob fell to the floor, and a millisecond later, the ripples of the glass seized. The glass exploded outwards towards the backyard. Getting to his feet, Bob swayed a little as Malcolm picked up the dining room table like it weighed nothing.

'Bob, watch out!'

Swinging the table like a bat as Bob turned, Malcolm swatted Bob like a fly. Standing helpless, I screamed as Bob flew passed me and smashed into the wall of the lounge room. Unlike me, Bob didn't bounce off. He went through the wall and landed with a sickening crunch against the bathroom sink.

The mirror cracked behind his head, scarlet webs streaming through the reflective surface. Bob blinked at me, my shock and fear staring back at me. 'Vera.' He fell to the floor.

"No!"

A hand grabbed me and threw me to the ground. 'Move, and I will hurt you.'

Whimpering, I shrunk away from the threat. Stopping as my eyes caught his attention, Malcolm grabbed my chin and studied me. 'There is a wolf in there. I thought for sure that worthless mutt had lied about everything.'

Choking anger rose inside me. Howard betrayed his Alpha, betrayed his pack, betrayed my pack. As Malcolm punched handfuls of gyprock so he could climb through the wall, the anger hit me.

Malcolm was going to kill Bob. Bob was going to die for trying to protect me, and I was sitting here doing nothing like the pathetic weak human. He was my pack, they had taken me in, cared for me, shown me not all our kind were assholes. Why couldn't I protect him?

The need to do something burbled up in me like water boiling in my veins. The bubbles of rage and loyalty growing bigger and bigger as the anger burnt away my fear. Lifting my head as Malcolm broke his way through the wall, I focused on Bob lying in human form on the other side. A crumpled heap of flesh and blood and glistening white bits I swear was bone. As Malcolm shifted to human form, my need to protect my pack reached the boiling point.

'Vera!' Dale was somewhere far away, his fear coating my tongue like a mouthful of dough.

Refusing to swallow his fear for me, I let my focus stay on my bathroom, ignoring the itching all over my body. The pack came first. Bob was pack.

As Malcolm readied to break Bob's neck, my instinct exploded from me in a shower of strawberry cream fur. Launching from where I was, through the hole in the wall, my jaws latched on Malcolm's neck.

The animal snarled, gave a sharp turn of its head, reefing Malcolm's head to the side. Then blood, glorious blood was filling my mouth and nose, coating, and washing away the dough of fear. My claws raked at flesh as we tumbled through the bathroom door into the bedroom. With a good grip his throat, I yanked my head to one side and felt everything in my mouth tear away from its restraint. Spitting the flesh and sinew out, I dove back in. Angry claws raked down my back. The stench of fear cloyed my senses as I wrapped my jaws around muscle, cartilage, veins, and nerves. I wrenched again.

The satisfying rip thrilled me, the spray of blood like a geyser showered me with praise. Still, those claws burned, ripping chunks of fur and flesh from my back. I didn't care. I needed to protect my pack, my cub, my life.

Biting down a third time, I jerked away with a sloppy rip, pop, gurgle, and the claws of the beast beneath me fell away. The geysers of victory lost their power and turned into puddles on the floor.

Backing away, checking, making sure. The beast trembled violently. The murky brown fur stained in blood withdrew, leaving the man who abused me looking into the next world.

Awareness flooded my brain, and I backed away faster. In the bathroom, I moved to a rapidly blinking Bob. Sniffing my packmate, I was careful where my paws fell. Crouching low, I shuffled closer, investigating the fading focus of his eyes.

Lifting a hand, Bob patted my neck. He was so weak, I barely felt it. "It's okay, Vera. You are safe now. He can never hurt you again."

Whimpering, I scooched forward nuzzling him.

"It's okay." His hand fell to the floor.

Sitting up, I cried, screaming my pain, baying to the moon to save my packmate.

The front door kicked open, followed by a stampede of feet. Turning towards the new threat, I growled. Jeremy appeared. Taking in the scene, he rushed forward. Backing up into the corner of the bathroom, I tried to get out of his way.

Dale was right behind him, eyes searching for me. When the indigo-gold irises found me, relief flooded my entire being. Trembling, I reached for him. As I did, my muscles tensed and released. My paw elongated and formed into a hand, my arm followed. I stepped out of the wolf as I moved towards Dale. As if a forcefield stood between us, and as I passed through the invisible barrier, I emerged human.

Jeremy was on the phone as he tended Bob's wounds. Taking my hand, Dale moved me out of the way. Guiding me from the room, Dale led me away from the lump of flesh and blood that had once been my tormenter.

From the lounge room, I watched Jeremy assess all of Bob's injuries. After a tense few moments, Jeremy exhaled. "None of them are fatal. Blood transfusion and stitches, and he will heal." Glancing to the corner I'd huddled in, Jeremy frowned. That's when I noticed the blood. "Is she hurt badly?"

"Torn up and will need stitches."

Flinching, I realized that while I worried about Bob, Dale was examining the damage to my back.

"You healed a fair bit when you shifted, Vera. Bob did too."

Shaking off the fog in my head, I took Dale's hand and stared at him with my mouth hanging open.

Reading my expression, a small smile of pride lit up his eyes. "I know, I felt it too," he murmured and rubbed my nose with his.

"I felt you, your need to protect Bob. It gave me the courage to find my wolf. I feel you, Dale."

Looking beyond relieved, Dale pulled me into his arms, and I sensed the emotional turmoil inside him. Relief that I didn't deny the bond any longer. Pride for being able to shift to animal form and back without his help. Concern for Bob - we shared that one, but my fear was trumping his because guilt buoyed it up. Anger.

"You're upset with me?"

"I told you to run. I meant out the door, not at him."

Peering over his shoulder, I could see Malcolm's leg, but nothing more. "I needed to protect my pack more than you needed me to be safe. Protecting my chance at being safe, and my chance to be happy meant more to me than anything else in the world."

Dale kissed my forehead. "If I couldn't feel it, Vera, I would be so angry with you right now. But I understand." Taking my face in his hands, Dale forced me to meet his eyes. "I understand."

CHAPTER 25

Forty-one stitches in my back and I wasn't allowed to complain about a single one because bob had it worse. I could have complained, but I wouldn't. Those shiny white bits I'd seen on Bob in the bathroom, they were bone. After Jonathan patched us up, Dale forced Bob to shift to full-wolf. After an hour of recovery, he then made Bob come back to human, to help speed the healing process.

Me, no. No more shifting for me for a while. Jonathan declared it too dangerous. Patched up, they took us back to the main house. My cottage swarmed by the pack, all coming to their Alpha's call. There were twice as many as I thought, which was three times the size of Malcolm's. Dale must have called them in case Malcolm hadn't come alone, but he had.

It took Dale wrapping my robe around my shoulders before I even realized I was still naked. Images like a puzzle flashing in my mind telling me that I hadn't been the only one. There weren't many men who could have stayed calm in this situation. Finding their wife naked with three naked guys. Albeit, two of them dead, and the third badly mangled. It was like a macabre orgy.

That night, I slept in Dale's arms, though, sleep may be the wrong word. Tossing and turning, I fought Malcolm off over and over again in my head. The next morning, before breakfast, Dale took me back to the cottage and stood me over Malcolm's body.

"He's dead, Vera. He can never hurt you again. You need to see this, let it sink in." Dale stepped back from me. "Do what you need to do to make it real for you." While Dale giving me space, but he was paying attention and staying close if I needed him.

Tears fell down my cheeks as I stared down at the body. Years upon years of pain and fear. "He said it wasn't all bad. He said until my pheromones became too much, they were nice to me."

Staring at Malcolm, painful moment after painful moment got washed away to one moment. It all came down to one horrible deed. "He raped a fourteen-year-old virgin and acted like I should be grateful. Every time he touched me, he was raping me all over again, for years, and he convinced me that this is how it is. That this is what it is like for women."

Dale growled, a thread of his fury whipping through the room, but I didn't cringe from it. Dale's anger no longer terrified me, it soothed me. Feeling his rage at my experience, reassured me that it wasn't the typical male mentality.

"I know I'm not the first, and I won't be the last. Human or otherwise. It should never happen. What it does is more than physical. It lasts longer than the act takes for him, and it's more than forcing you against your will."

My fingers were cramping as the pain and torment of that one unforgivable deed called my hate to the surface. With a scream worthy of a horror film, I lunged. Clawing at his face, his chest, gouging out his eyes, ripping his heart and lungs from his chest. Tearing away his sense of self like he did to me.

I wanted my hate to stain his soul. For Malcolm to know how it felt not to be able to breathe around the anguish of you, as a person, not mattering. For him to experience being a body, a piece of flesh for amusement.

There was an unsatisfying lack of blood - since the body exsanguinated the night before. Still, the ruined body, his torn-up face, his sightless eyes, it didn't take it away. Nothing ever was going too.

Closing my eyes, I cried for a minute. My claws cramped, and I stretched them as they returned to human form. Washing my hands and face, I stared at the scarlet veined webbing of my shattered mirror. Bob nearly died protecting me.

"They are not all bad, but they aren't all good." My eyes drifted to the corner where Howard's body was still slumped. "Even amongst the good, there are the rotten." Sucking in a breath, I walked out to find Dale struggling to control his emotions on the back veranda. Tears stained his cheeks, and it made my heart skip a beat that his empathy extended that deep.

"It's devastating, and the effects will last a lifetime. It is like having your entire self, body, and soul, eviscerated." I considered the back-yard. "He never got that. I doubt he cared enough to even try."

My sense of Dale evoked torn emotions. He wanted to wrap me up and assure me that would never happen to me again. He also accepted touching me right now may not sit well with me. Another part of him wanted to go back in and finish maiming Malcolm's body. Dale wanted to throw the body to his pack and watch them play tug-a-war with it, ripping it to a thousand pieces.

As voices approached from the forest path, Dale lifted his head to watch the Liderii arrive. There were strange wolves with them. Moving to Dale as he composed himself, I used my sleeve to wipe the remnants of his sympathy away. Threading my fingers with his, I gazed into his eyes. "That was my past; you are my future."

Smiling, Dale cupped my face and kissed me. His eyes looked between us, then back to meet mine. "I have to tell them."

Understanding it was necessary, I nodded. "I'm going to go back to the house, check on Bob, and cook him something special for breakfast."

Clamping my hand in his before I could walk away, Dale collected his phone, texting as he talked. "Greet them first, it is important. Jeremy will come down to walk you back to the house."

More than happy to not be alone right now, I stayed close to Dale's side. Last night, Dale told me that from now on, if he was in the city, so was I. Since, I didn't like being away from him, I didn't mind.

We greeted the Liderii as friends. Quinton was very concerned with my wellbeing. "I hear congratulations were in order before this sadness? The Goddess asks her chosen to endure so much, but the happiness she grants them as a reward is beyond compare."

Thinking back to the story of Luna and the tragedy that befell her before she found her mate, it made me hope. Cerese was beside herself with the idea of an Alpha trying to steal another Alpha's mate. But it was Ralph who got down to business.

"We will need to notify his pack. By law, you should be their new Alpha, Dale."

"I didn't kill him; I can't take the credit."

"Who's...?"

"Vera can shift, to both beast and full form. She protected her new packmate, she saved Bob's life."

The Liderii stared at me. Thankfully, Jeremy arrived at that moment. "I need to rest and check on Bob. I will make you all morning tea for when you finish."

"Vera is an accomplished chef. It is worth experiencing," Dale encouraged.

"I look forward to it," Quinton replied. "I would also like to see you try and teach Cerese to shift, as you did your wife."

"Could he do that?" I whispered to Jeremy.

"He is a strong alpha. It is worth the try. If he can teach Cerese, he might be able to teach Alexia and Hymn, and then the other half-breeds."

Considering what it would be like for all these girls to find their wolf after all this time. "That would be pretty awesome."

"The twins would think so."

"How is Bob this morning?"

"Whining. More so because until he heals, he can't see Juliet. Too hard to explain. So, he's annoyed about how long he has to wait until he gets laid."

That answer was a weight off my mind. "He's going to be okay."

"Yes, he will. And so are you." Jeremy placed his arm around my shoulders. It shocked him more than me when I let him. He was so happy.

Stopping mid-step, I stared at Jeremy wide-eyed. "I can feel you, feel your emotions, like I do Dale."

For the first time, Jeremy smiled shyly. "We are pack, Vera. You mated with Dale to get your bond. But when you protected Bob last night, when you recognized him as your pack, you forged the pack bond with us all. That is what brought all the pack here last night, not Dale. They heard and responded to your cry for help for Bob."

Smiling, I threw my arms around his neck. "You're my family. I never had this with the other pack."

Moving me back to see my face, Jeremy frowned. "What, at all? Not even before Malcolm killed your father?" When I shook my head, Jeremy looked curious. "That is unusual, Vera."

"Welcome to my life."

Reaching the house, I smiled as we stepped inside and made our way to the kitchen.

"What's wrong?" Jeremy asked when I stopped and grinned.

"This is my baby now. Dale may be the Alpha, but in my kitchen, I'm the boss."

Snickering, Jeremy lowered his voice to a smooth tenor. "I'll be sure to let Dale know you're on top in the kitchen."

Biting my lip at the desire coming off him, I stepped back. "I thought you weren't affected by my pheromones now?"

Jeremy laughed. "Oh, I'm not. But, you are still a beautiful female, Vera. A man can dream."

"Not about me, you can't."

"Don't worry, no one in the pack will act on it. You'll always be safe with us now. Even if anything happens to Dale."

"I thought if one of a mated pair dies, so does the other?"

Frowning a little, Jeremy rubbed my upper arms. "If you died, it would kill Dale, yes. Not instantly, but his broken heart would see him follow you soon after. For she-wolfs it doesn't work the same. You will grieve him, but the pack will buoy you up, especially if you have cubs, you will be able to survive his loss. After some time, you may choose to mate with the new Alpha or give your soul to the moon to be with your mate. Either way, the bond isn't what kills mates, it's their broken hearts."

"Wait, wouldn't you be the new Alpha?"

"Hence, why I still find you attractive, Vera. If anything ever happens to Dale, it will be my instinct to take his place and take care of you."

"And by taking care of me, you mean take care of yourself."

Snickering, Jeremy walked away. Sighing, I went to check on Bob, who was only concerned with making sure that I was okay. That conversation got nowhere. Resigning myself to the kitchen, I cooked Bob breakfast and something for our guests.

Jeremy was licking the bowl clean when Dale led the Liderii inside. "Jeremy, if you go with Ralph's beta, they are going to deliver the body along with the summons. You can request what you were asking about at the same time."

Popping his finger from his mouth, Jeremy took the clean bowl to the sink. "Leave it, I'll wash it up." Giving me a kiss to the temple, Jeremy put the bowl aside and disappeared with one of Ralph's men.

Chuckling at the look on my face from Jeremy's affection, Dale directed the Liderii to the lounge. Cerese came to talk with me instead.

"What is it like?"

Lifting my eyes from my prep-work for dinner, I considered her question. "Like every part of your body is cramping, and your muscles are crushing the bones they wrap around. To ease it, I focused on stretching out the cramp, and as I stretched, I changed."

Cerese was wide-eyed. "And you took full-form?"

"That was when I took beast. The first time I took wolf-form was last night. It happened while I was focusing on saving Bob, so I actually didn't feel the shift. I was me one minute and on four paws the next."

"Were you scared?" She was so thrilled by the prospect, but I sensed her anxiety too.

"Yes." Dale didn't warn me, so I had no idea what was happening until it was in play. Remembering the second time we did it and how I was eager, I leaned over the bench. "Dale's jealous. In beast form, I grow a full bushy tail. The males don't get tails in beast form."

"No, they don't. Ralph would go nuts if I grew a tail."

"I know, Dale did. I could barely walk the next day from him enjoying my tail."

Cerese gaped, then she started chortling. "I hope it works."

"When are you going to try?"

"Tonight, before we head home," she was biting her fingernails.

Grabbing a carrot stick, I handed it to her. "Your nails are too pretty to gnaw on."

"Ladies," Dale interrupted. "Could you join us?"

When Dale offered me his hand, I packed my prep-work in the fridge and went with him. Leading me to the lounge, Dale wrapped his arms around me from behind.

"As you all know, Vera has changed to both beast and wolf. What we discovered last night when she took full-form, is that while in beast form, Vera conceived. She's going to have my cub."

CHAPTER 26

"*Y*ou look quite pensive," Dale chuckled to himself as he came in his bedroom. Approaching where I sat on the window seat at the bay window, Dale glanced past my shoulder. "Did you watch the show?"

Focusing my eyes back to where Ralph and Cerese were doing the wild thing in beast form, I observed them. "It was harder for her, and for you."

Pulling me to him, Dale was already naked, having revealed his own beast to help Cerese reach her own. "I am not bonded with Cerese. I am not her Alpha. The only reason I could do what I did is that I am the strongest Alpha to ever exist in memory."

"Maybe the Goddess always gives us one, to ensure we have our guide to our true nature?"

"You are my mate, Vera. I've waited over a hundred years for you to enter my life. I hope to have a hundred more with you." Stroking the hair back from my face, Dale gazed into my eyes. "Have you had any dreams that would indicate that won't be the case?"

"I barely slept last night, and Malcolm dead changes my future."

"No, Vera. This baby and I, we were always your future. The day I sank fang into you, the day we bonded, you told me I would give you a baby. You saw the future then." His hand covered my tummy. "That hasn't changed."

Swiping the tears from my eyes, I stared down at my tummy in awe. When I lifted my gaze, Dale smiled down at my tears of happiness. He dropped his mouth to mine, but I pulled back. "Won't they need you to help shift her back?"

"She grew a tail. I know what your tail did to me. They'll be a while yet."

Laughing as Dale picked me up and sat back on the bed, I straddled his naked lap. His thick erection knocked against my protected womanhood. "How do you think your kids will take the news?"

Lifting my dress over my head, Dale cupped my breasts. "They will be thrilled. Alexa and Hymn more so if I can teach them to at least reach their beast."

"Because they could increase their chance of conception?"

"That hasn't is only a theory."

"I'm pretty sure Cerese and Ralph are trying to prove it right now."

Dale gifted me a sly smile. "True, but we shouldn't get the girls' hopes up." He was such a protective dad, and I was falling deeper and deeper for him. "I'm only willing to try bringing the girls to their beast because they can both already shift their eyes and hands. They are my daughters, so they were born stronger than most of our females."

"Is Cameron stronger than most?"

"Yes."

"Then why isn't Cameron your Beta?"

"Because he wants his own pack, Vera. He wants to breed and be his own Alpha, and he should because he is strong enough."

"He hasn't gotten anyone knocked up yet?"

"Not from lack of trying, I assure you. Most women of quality, who are free with their bodies, practice safe sex, and use birth control. So, for the chance at building his pack, Cameron would have to marry. So far, he hasn't found a woman to who he is willing to commit."

"Never stopped you, and that was in the age of chastity and virtue."

Dale got an evil smirk on his face, the look deliciously sinful, and I swear my knickers melted right off my body. "I didn't say Cameron hasn't been a dog in the past, he is very much his father's son."

"But no children?"

"One conceived, almost fifty years ago." Dale stopped the story. "How is your back?"

Sensing his unease and his concern for me, I also picked up it had nothing to do with my injuries. "Tight. Jonathan will need to take the stitches out tomorrow. It feels healed already."

Slipping out from under me, Dale stood behind me to observe my back. "No, you have healed faster than he expected. I'll call him to come over now."

When Dale went to collect the phone, I grabbed his wrist, surprising Dale with how fast I moved. "Tell me the rest. I am not fragile, Dale. I can take hearing that bad shit happened to other people, or are you worried I will hate Cameron."

Forehead furrowing, Dale contemplated me. "Let me call Jonathan, then I will tell you the rest."

Removing my hand from his wrist, Dale made the call while I pulled my dress back on. Once he set the phone down, Dale sat beside me on the bed.

"Cameron would have married her. When he went to her father to seek permission to propose, the father refused. The father came after Cameron to kill him. He didn't succeed, and instead, lost his own life."

"The daughter blamed Cameron?"

Dale shook his head. "The father had beaten the girl before he came after Cameron. When he beat his daughter to cause a miscarriage, he caused massive internal damage."

Sucking in a painful breath, my hand covered my tummy out of instinct. "He killed her?"

Taking my hand in his, Dale squeezed it in comfort. "His daughter died with her child, while her murderer paid for his sins."

"That affected Cameron?"

"Despite not loving her, Cameron mourned the girl. More so, he had already given his heart to the child inside her. Cameron fears to cause such heartache again."

We sat there for several moments. "Dale, make love to me."

Kissing my cheek, Dale breathed in through his nose as he pulled back to my ear. "As soon as Jonathan has left, I will lay you on this bed and make love to you until the dawn comes."

Squirming at the thought, I shook my head. "I can't be that patient."

When Dale chuckled, the sound flipped my stomach. "You make me so happy, Vera." Pulling me back into his lap, I pulled my knickers aside and nestled him in my warm cocoon.

"Dale, I don't want to be happy, I want you to make me ecstatic."

His laugh brightened up my insides. Dale's smile was a lighthouse on the rocky shores of my past, guiding me to calmer waters. Gripping my hips, Dale leaned back, his abs contracting to hold him at an angle so I could take him deeper.

"Dale?" Jeremy called walking in the room.

"Go away," I panted on the brink of nirvana.

"Sorry!" Jeremy cringed, but his sudden desire to join in rammed against me as if his body rubbed up against me.

My eyes flew open, Dale held me tight as Jeremy stepped back out muttering about shutting the door. "Take it as a compliment, Vera, not a threat. Jeremy would never harm you."

Swallowing my alarm, I closed my eyes to focus. Reopening them, I saw Dale holding a baby in his arms, singing nursery rhymes. His indigo eyes came to me, bright and happy before they dropped lower. Glancing down, I smiled at the baby I held in my arms. Happiness beyond anything I'd ever experienced radiated out of me.

Throwing back my head as my body seized, I cried out my pleasure. Not only of the body but of my heart and soul.

Dale cradled me to him, both of us breathing heavy. "Twins. I'm carrying twins."

Pulling back, Dale's face filled with wonder. Kissing me with utmost passion, Dale flipped me onto my stomach and pounded me from behind. His hips bucked while his fingers held me lovingly restrained. As my nails dragged the comforter across the bed, I cried out my physical pleasure again. Dale announced his joy to the house.

"Twins!"

Feeling it in my bones, in my very being, I knew he had notified the entire pack of my condition. Panting, I started laughing.

Hesitating a moment, Dale fell to the bed laughing beside me. "Sorry. I got a bit excited."

Climbing onto his chest, I started kissing him. He made my insides feel bright with happiness. I couldn't believe how much my life had changed overnight. How light and bright my life was now. Knowing why, I redirected my thoughts because I didn't want to think about that anymore. Malcolm had stolen fourteen years with pain and misery. I was devoting the rest of it to happiness.

"I'm starving."

Smiling at me as I went to the bathroom to clean up, Dale wolf-whistled, his eyes drinking me up. Pure desire and happiness radiated from him. A moment later, he joined me in the shower.

"Jonathan is here, and Ralph and Cerese have finished experimenting. I'll help Ralph bring his wife back to human form while you get those stitches out. Then, you should eat while I speak to Jeremy."

Kissing him deeply, I let him go. When I finished showering, I emerged to find Jonathan waiting in the bedroom. "Have you checked on Bob?"

"He's next; you first."

Lying down on the bed, stomach down, Jonathan opened the towel to start his work.

"So, twins. Do we know the sex?"

"No. They were both wrapped in white."

"Well, I've given Jeremy the brand of a good antenatal vitamin supplement I want you to start taking. It will ensure you and the babies are well-nourished."

After Jonathan finished, I dressed and moved out to the kitchen for food. My steps slowed when I heard Dale talking. "And we are sure this relates to her?"

"It is the old Alpha's diary. The Beta gave it up without issue and have accepted the Liderii summons. None of them seemed torn up about losing Malcolm. We explained the cause of their exceptional violence for the last ten years. They are most repentant."

"So, she was never theirs. That is why none of them even tried to protect her. She was never pack."

Stepping into the room, my heart was beating a million miles per hour because I knew he was talking about me.

"Your suspicions were correct. He stole her."

Sensing me, Dale stood up. Turning his head, Jeremy bowed it in sadness. When Dale held out his arms, I went to him, letting him wrap me up. I always knew I didn't belong there. I always knew I wasn't one of them. After holding me for several minutes, Dale sat us down and indicated Jeremy explain.

"When you revealed you never felt connected to your pack, I asked the Liderii to summons the old Alpha's papers. Your old pack is complying out of fear of retribution for breaking tradition."

Jeremy held up a ledger. "This is a registry of births in the pack. You aren't in it."

"My real name -"

"You aren't in it. No female is." Placing the ledger down, Jeremy picked up another. "This is the Alpha's diary. It is required by our law that every Alpha keeps one."

"Really? You aren't worried the humans would get hold of them?"

"We keep them safe," Dale assured, while Jeremy leafed through it.

"Based on your age, I only had to search a few to find the right year." Opening a page, Jeremy cleared his throat.

Holding up his hand, Dale sat forward. "Wait! Cerese and Ralph should hear this. Vera, you need to eat."

A little annoyed at having to wait, but starving enough to shut up, I raided the fridge. The entire time, I wondered what the diary revealed about me. Maybe my parents still lived. Fixing snacks, I'd made enough for a party by the time Dale came to the kitchen and bundled me up in his arms first.

"Calm down. I know you are anxious, but this is not going to be a happy tale."

After carrying everything to the dining table, Dale made everyone wait until I had eaten. Instead, Dale spoke about another person. "Do you remember Jacob, Ralph?"

"Yes, of course. What happened to him was horrible."

"Who was he?"

Eyes falling on me, Ralph sighed. "A former alpha who once was also a member of the Liderii. He died almost thirty years ago now."

"How?"

Taking my hand as I sat back, Dale seemed satisfied with what I'd eaten. "Pelt hunters. They mistook him for a pure wolf and killed him. Since he was Lycan, he reverted to a human at death so they couldn't take the pelt. The hunters reported it as an accidental killing. They shot what they thought was a wolf and turned out to be a man running naked through the woods."

"Why did you bring it up?" Ralph queried.

"It's relevant." Dale gestured for Jeremy to begin.

Jeremy picked up the diary. "The routine patrol revealed the scent of trespassers. Human's, with weapons. We recognized the smell of death that followed them. Chasing it, we were eager to drive them from our territory and teach them a lesson in hunting wolves.

"The hunt took us out of our territory. We considered turning back but decided to hunt a little farther. We wanted to see if we could determine where they came from, so we could keep watch. That is when we heard it. A child crying. I sent the others to spread out, to ensure it wasn't a trap. The child cried and cried. When I felt it was safe, I approached.

"She sat naked, covered in blood, besides the two naked bodies of her parents. At first, I thought something sinister had taken place. That humans killed this couple and left the child for nature to destroy. But, the child didn't fear me. In fact, when I came close enough, she clung to me as if I should give her comfort.

"That is when I caught their scent. The parents were not human, they were Lycan. Observing them, I recognized the man as Alpha Jacob, who left the Luna Shadows pack for the honor of the Liderii. Beside him, was a female Lycan I didn't know, but I understood, at that moment, that she had been a wolf when shot. White fur littered the ground where the bullet shredded her.

"My attention returned to the girl. Clinging to me like I would save her. Sniffing her, she smelled like earth and forest, and of night and moonlight. She was one of us. A female, born of a mother who could shift. I wondered if the child had been a cub when her parents died, and she followed them into human form.

"Shifting, I collected the child up and returned home with her. I didn't tell the others what I suspected. I needed to contact the Liderii first, needed to secure the child a good home. My pack is not the place for her. I don't trust my Beta. There are too many untrustworthy looks, and my sense of him has faded. I need to get this child somewhere safe before I am challenged. She has seen enough death for her short life. I have called Quinton and left a message for him to call me back."

Closing the diary, Jeremy put it aside. The table was quiet. Dale squeezed my hand.

"He intended to contact you, why didn't he?"

Passing the diary to Ralph, Jeremy took a deep breath. "That was the last entry of Alpha Sam. When he returned home that evening, his Beta didn't challenge him, he killed him in a craven attack in his study. Immediately after Sam made that entry.

"One of the elders told me Sam arrived with the girl and no explanation. He was in his study with her for thirty minutes waiting for a phone call when the Beta murdered his Alpha. The Delta, disgusted by the Beta's underhanded tactic, challenged the Beta and bested him. He showed the disgraced Beta, no mercy."

"That was the alpha who raised you, Vera," Dale informed me. "And Malcolm was the spineless Beta's bastard son. The new Alpha never let him live down his father's cowardice, and Malcolm let it eat away at his very being."

Malcolm's hatred for the Alpha he bested swarmed all over me again. "His treatment of me was his vengeance on the man who killed his father and made his childhood hell?"

Dale embrace me, comforting me as that rocky shoreline threatened to tear me apart again. Greedy human hunters, a coward of a Beta, and his vengeful son destroyed my life.

With my tears staining his shirt, Dale lifted me into his arms and bid everyone goodnight as he took me back to his room. Crying all night, I grieved for my parents and for the life I lost. Dale held me tight through it all.

As the sun rose in the morning, I lifted my swollen eyes to see Dale watching me. When I traced his lips with my finger, Dale dropped his mouth and kissed me, with a fierce and unbridled passion. He showed me all the reasons it was going to be okay.

Clinging to my lighthouse, I held tight while he guided me back to safe waters. As the storm in my heart calmed to reveal the bright future before us, I thanked the Goddess for gifting me a home.

EPILOGUE

"Okay, I've got an hour until dale has his next meeting. Let's play." Turning on the music, I picked up my camera. Dale had given me my own and paid for me to do classes to improve my ability. While the underground media was my main contract, I filled in if needed for other shoots.

The model and talent agency weren't Dale's only business, it was the one he put his face behind and ran daily. Everything editorials needed for publication, one of Dale's companies produced. So, if his models were on a shoot, and the photographer the client hired didn't show, Dale would offer my services. Provided it wasn't Wednesday or the weekend.

Wednesday mornings, I traveled home with Jeremy and back to the city with Dale on Thursday mornings. Friday nights, I drove back with Dale.

"Did you want us to keep going?"

Taking the camera away, I lifted a brow at Adam. "You read the request, didn't you?"

Cheeky grin in place, Adam mimicked my raised brow. "Yes. I also remember the last time we did a transformation fuck scene and how you reacted."

"I'd like to point out I am no longer pregnant. There is no chance of me going into labor today. I may need to finish early, so I have enough time to fuck my husband before his next meeting, but I won't go into labor."

Adam and Hymn laughed. "Come on, Adam, let's see if you can get me knocked up."

"I don't want to be alpha, and I'm happy in my pack, thank you."

Smiling, I shook my head. Those two were everything but married. They still slept with others, but they always came back to each other. My camera clicked as Hymn acted out the scene. Transforming into her beast, she attacked Adam.

Word had gotten around the packs that a Lycan female took out a violent Alpha. Now females going beast and all but raping the men was the fantasy. Personally, it sickened me, so I tried to tune it out. Feeling the same, Alexia refused to take part. She'd do the beast sex if it were mutual, but she left the rough stuff to Hymn.

Speaking of violent. "Hymn!" Standing up, I took a step forward as she got carried away. "Look to me."

Focusing on me, Hymn snarled up at me as she rode Adam, who was playing with her breasts. A tingle in the air was all the warning I got as Adam lost control and his beast came on him.

Stepping back, I checked my photos while those two rolled around on the floor. Grabbing my bag, I left them there. Making sure I locked the door on the way out, so no one walked in on them, I made my way back up to Dale's office.

When I arrived back early, Jeremy looked confused. "That was quick, is something wrong?"

"Adam lost control of his beast."

Taking the camera, Jeremy huffed. "Again? It's already taken three hours this morning."

"Yeah, but this time he lasted long enough for me to get the shot."

As Jeremy plugged the camera into his computer, I came around the desk to look over his shoulder. Pulling the pictures up, I pointed to the one that fit the brief. "That one."

Clicking it to full screen, Jeremy smiled. "Perfect."

BOUNDARY

"The close-ups of Hymn are good too. She was verging on a full shift."

"She can't do a full shift."

"Compare this photo with this photo."

Noting the two I pointed at, Jeremy's mouth fell open. I slapped his shoulder. "Told you. It's been over a year, it's so easy for me now, and I've only been shifting for six months. She's gotten more fluid with her shift and is starting to push for the next level. Give it a few more months, she'll be able to go wolf too."

Mouth hanging open, Jeremy shook his head. "That would be amazing."

"When she does, I think Adam and her will realize they are mates."

"What?" Jeremy's eyes bulged as I pushed through into Dale's office.

Sitting at his desk writing notes while on the phone, Dale smiled in my direction, and lifted a brow at the time. Giving him the thumbs up, I went to the port-a-cot in the corner. Tucking Jacob's blanket around him better, I smiled as Stephanie gurgled in her sleep.

"Okay, I'll get on that." Hanging up the phone, Dale typed an email. "You got the shot?"

"Yes." Turning to face him, I surveyed my husband and bit my lip. "I'm horny."

"I can feel that."

"The babies are still sleeping. The email could wait ten minutes."

"We've discussed the work boundary."

Rolling my eyes, I pulled my top over my head and dropped it to the floor. My pants went immediately after so I was standing in my underwear. Clearing his throat, Dale continued typing. Walking to his lounge, I laid myself down. "I'm going to have a rest then."

Dale's raised brow told me that he didn't believe me, but he didn't say anything. Getting comfortable, I started touching myself.

"Vera."

Ignoring him, I kept making myself feel nice. The growl when I moaned the first time only encouraged me. It wasn't until I slipped a finger inside me, that Dale couldn't stand by and watch anymore.

Appearing above me, Dale relieved me of my underwear. Bowing his head between my thighs, he tasted my need for himself.

When I moaned, Dale chuckled. "You'll wake the babies again."

Snatching the cushion, I held it over my face.

Every time we found time to be intimate, the babies woke up. I don't think it was my moaning and more their knowledge that mummy and daddy were having fun. It was no different to when I sat down to eat. I could have fed them both, but if I put a piece of food between my teeth, they woke up and needed me.

Moaning again, I threw the pillow away as I grabbed Dale and kissed him. "I can't wait." Throwing him on the floor, I climbed on top of him. "I haven't cum in three days. I need to cum, Dale."

Dale was trying not to laugh as I freed his hard-on and climbed on board. As he slid inside, pure relief escaped my lips in a sigh.

"Goddess, I love you. But I miss how often we had sex before the babies came."

Struggling to keep his eyes open, Dale bit his lip on a growl. As controlled as he behaved, and as much restraint as he tried to show, he missed it as much as I did. "This is normal, Vera. Babies change the dynamics."

"I'm happy for them to change the dynamics all they want, as long as it doesn't stop us practicing for more, at least once a day. Maybe twice."

Groaning, Dale helped my hips rock over him. "At least." He was so close; I wasn't the only one denied their happy ending of late.

Closing my eyes, I let the pleasure build. My body was racing for the prize, desperate to get there before one or two of my precious cubs opened their eyes. Dropping my mouth to Dale's shoulder to mute my moans, the change of angle worked for both of us.

Panting with the biggest grin on my face, I rested my cheek on his clothed chest. "That's the third time we've had sex in your office, and they've not woken up."

"They do seem to sleep well here."

"The room smells of you. More so than our bedroom at the apartment or even at home."

"I do spend all day here five days a week. Granted, I'm in and out, but I come back here more than any other place."

"Then it's settled. Clear your calendar for their afternoon sleeps for four days a week.

Dropping his head back, Dale laughed. "I don't remember my last wife being this demanding."

Huffing, I rolled off him. "I'm not going to acknowledge that. I'm not your last wife, I am your mate, and it's entirely different."

"Yes, it is." Caressing my cheek, Dale kissed me, with all the feeling in his heart. His eyes flicked towards the cot as he rolled on top of me again. "We should use this time well."

Gasping a laugh as he pushed inside me, I came twice more before we fell to the floor panting and wheezing. I couldn't stop smiling.

Collecting his clothes from the floor, Dale looked at his watch as a knock sounded at the door. "Crap! Tell Jeremy I'll be five minutes." Dale dashed into his bathroom as I rolled onto my stomach, and the door opened.

"He'll be five minutes, Jeremy."

"I'll call and tell them he's stuck in another meeting and should be there in ten."

"Thank you. And can you move any appointments he has for tomorrow at this time? I need quality wife time."

Trying very hard not to grin and failing, Jeremy pressed his lips together. "I'll see what I can do."

Naked as a jaybird in the middle of the floor, I was nearly asleep when a small smack landed on my rear, jolting me awake. "Shower while I dress."

With a groan, I dragged my tired and satisfied body to the shower. Doing enough to wash, I stepped out, dried, and dressed before slinking out to the office again.

Kissing me goodbye, Dale considered me with a frown. "Are you heading back to the apartment?"

"No. They are happy sleeping there, so I'm going to sleep on the couch while I can."

Caressing my face, Dale appraised my eyes. "If you need to rest, Alexia and Hymn said they would babysit a few hours."

Smiling, I crashed onto the sofa. "Too tired to think, talk, walk…" I didn't even hear my head hit the pillow.

When I woke up, it was to the baby's giggling. Turning my head, I watched Hymn playing with them. When I closed my eyes, I saw her holding her own baby, Adam right there beside her. I didn't tell her. It wasn't for me to ruin the surprise. What the dream showed me was they wouldn't leave the pack, and that made me relieved.

Dale would miss his girls if they left. Cameron hadn't lived at the packhouse in years, but the girls were there when they weren't away working. Being honest, I'd miss them.

Yes, I was their stepmother, but we acted more like sisters, and they both adored Jacob and Steph. We'd all miss them if one of them left. Crawling over to the lounge, Jacob pulled himself up to standing. His indigo eyes smiled at me when he saw my eyes open.

In these moments, I forgot about the girl named Viridia, who went through so much. My children, Dale, the pack; the happiness of us all was all that mattered. Going forward, it was only going to get better.

ABOUT THE AUTHOR

Ebony lives in Sydney, Australia, with her husband, daughter, and six cats. She loves to read fantasy, thrillers, and paranormal romance, spending most of her free time with her nose in a book or writing.

Having always possessed an over-active imagination she spent her younger years regaling friends with fantastic stories, holding her audience captive with the passion and suspense of her characters plights.

Now in adulthood she has numerous published works and shows no signs of stopping her imagination from spreading across as many pages as it can find.

If you'd like to follow Ebony or simply say hi you can find her here:
Website: http://ebonyolson.com/

facebook.com/EbonyOlson.Author

twitter.com/Ebony_Olson

instagram.com/ebony_olson

goodreads.com/Ebony_Olson